TEN LESSONS TO DETERMINE MY FUTURE...

MASTER CLASS

LESSONS SEVEN AND EIGHT

paige press

Ten lessons to determine my future...

MASTER CLASS

Lessons Seven and Eight

RAVEN JAYNE

Paige Press
Leander, TX 78641

Ebook:
ISBN: 978-1-953520-97-5

Print:
ISBN: 978-1-953520-98-2

ALSO BY RAVEN JAYNE

MASTER CLASS

A collection of dirty, erotic novellas

Lesson One: Obey

Lesson Two: Tempt

Lesson Three: Take

Master Class: First Three Lessons

Lesson Four: Submit

Lesson Five: Offer

Lesson Six: Play

Master Class: Lessons Four, Five, Six

Lesson Seven: Trust

Lesson Eight: Break

Master Class: Lessons Seven and Eight

Lesson Nine: Master

Lesson Ten: Choose

ABOUT THIS BOOK

I've always been a good girl.
Doing what I'm told, doing the things I'm supposed to do.
I pride myself on being perfect.
My lessons have all been different, but they've taught me one thing above all--
If I don't ask for what I want, I won't get it.
It's time to forget about perfection.
Since God knows I can't forget about my desire for *him...*

TRUST

I learned something during my time away.

What *I* want. Not my husband, not my Master, not my father.

And I want something forbidden.

An affair with the man who trains me would never be allowed.

Especially not by the men who hired him.

But I know how to be persuasive...

1

JANE PROMISED me this place would be private, and it is —I'm surrounded by hedges, tucked into a corner of the local public park so that no one can see me. But I can hear people moving all around, talking to their dogs and each other, doing their everyday things—listening to music, beeping their cars open and closed, crunching leaves underfoot, reminding me of their presence over and over again, so that every time the breeze brushes against my bare arms, I feel even more and more vulnerable and exposed.

Jane says she and Bruce have fucked here a half-dozen times and never gotten caught; for her, the proximity of the rest of the world was part of the thrill. But for what I need to do today, I actually need that privacy —and I couldn't go to any of my usual places to get it. I couldn't go anywhere where I anyone I'd ever met in my little world would ever think to find me, or where they might see or overhear me, even by accident.

For most people who live in this city, this park is part of the texture of their everyday lives, but despite having lived just a few miles away for most of my life, I've never been here before. The neighborhood is much less nice than the one I grew up in, but still, glimpsing it through the window of a town car, I always thought it looked sort of shabby chic. Up close, though, it's much grittier than I'd imagined, spotted with signs reminding people to pick up their dog's poop and threatening them with arrests for dealing drugs. Stray pieces of trash flutter by, and my feet crush spent cigarette butts. I've never been anywhere this grimy before, and it makes me wonder if I could survive on my own in the real world.

I wonder what Malcolm will say about the setting when he arrives.

Malcolm. Even thinking his name feels like swallowing a shot of the best Russian vodka, sharp and cold down my throat, electricity along my spine. I asked him to meet me here early, before he'd be expected at the office—and then gave him a nice round number, the kind he never gave me, for our appointment out of pure uncut spite. It's 7:26 a.m. right now, which means I have four minutes until he comes striding up, eyes blazing, to ask what I think I'm up to.

I check one of the benches for anything too gross, and, when it passes inspection, gingerly take a seat. I close my eyes and take a deep breath, trying to steady and center myself. *Inhale, exhale. Inhale—*

A pigeon flutters up from under the bench and

scares the crap out of me. So much for calm and readiness.

I am definitely not cut out for the real world.

At 7:30 on the dot, he strides through an unassuming gap in the bushes. He's wearing his customary dark suit, his white shirt buttoned to the throat, tie impeccable, cufflinks gleaming, but I know better than to read his clothing for clues at this point. He'd be wearing this in a tornado or a hurricane. He'd wear it to dig ditches in the desert—and he wouldn't break a sweat.

Whether he's going to be Malcolm or Master with me today, I'll know as soon as he opens his mouth.

I don't even have to wait that long. I see it in his posture as he glances at me before taking a seat on the bench opposite, looking for all the world to anyone who didn't know him as well as I do like a businessman pausing to take a breath before getting to work.

What I can see that a casual observer couldn't is that, though he's just as powerful and commanding as always, tall and solid with purpose and intent, his reserve has softened just slightly. He's still brusque but not frigid, and when he leans forward and looks at me —really looks at me—his face is open, marked by a dark hunger that's shot through with tenderness. I feel that look in the marrow of my bones, and my body aches for his.

At first I thought I wanted Malcolm because I wanted everyone; my lessons awakened a craving I'd never known I possessed until men started touching me exactly the way I wanted to be touched, and I liked it more than I ever could have imagined. But it's different with Malcolm than it is with the rest of them, in ways I know better than to try to explain even to myself.

I'm fairly certain of who I'm meeting then, but there's one test that will let me know for certain. If I speak without being spoken to, Master will punish me.

Malcolm won't.

"Thank you for coming," I say.

His mouth twitches ever so slightly. He knows I'm playing a game with him, and he's going to let me, at least for now. So definitely Malcolm, then.

Good.

"I was curious why you picked this side of town," he says, after a moment.

"Why do you think?"

He leans back, stretching an arm over the back of his bench. I look at the broad line of his shoulders, the hard, flat plane of his belly, and I want to crawl between his knees and into his lap. I imagine the weight of his hand on my head, warm and soft, but still commanding, holding me in place for him, and my pussy is so wet my panties are soaked through.

"Now that I'm here, I get it," he says. "I could take you to the middle of Franklin Boulevard, right over there, past those trees... I could push you up against the streetlight pole, and fuck you like a savage...just the way you like it...and a hundred people could see, but no one would know who we were."

My cheeks are hot with shame and want. Of course he knows. Malcolm always knows what I want, often even before I do. "Pretty much."

"Or I could take you right here and a hundred people wouldn't see, and even if one did…"

God, if he keeps speaking I'm going to do it: get down on my hands and knees and suck his cock in the park like a whore. Sit on his lap and slide his dick inside of me so fast he doesn't have time to make me stop, and then let him fuck me as roughly as he wants as a punishment. I have to make him stop winding me up like this. "I just wanted to talk," I say.

"Well, here I am. What do you want?"

"Glad you asked." I take another deep, long breath before I dive in. I'm nervous—terrified, actually, maybe more terrified than I've ever been in my life, including when I explored underwater caves near Bali, or when I rode nervy, poorly-trained horses at some minor duke's country estate in Lausanne. But I have to do this. The only thing that scares me more than having this conversation is what will happen if I don't.

"I don't know what's going on in your life," I begin. "I don't know what you do when you're not with me, or who you fuck or why you fuck them." I make sure to look him in the eye, bold and direct, when I say, "I know why you fucked me. It was business. But I don't know why you helped me with the chess, and I don't know why you came to my room, and told me your name, and said what you said."

Another deep breath. That part was almost easy—

I've been wanting to ask Malcolm questions since the moment I met him. This last part is the most recent, and so it's going to be the hardest. I'm going to ask him for something I'm not at all sure he'll give me.

"I've been doing nothing but trying to figure that out," I say, "and then I realized it doesn't matter why you did what you did as much as it matters what I want. And what I want is you, Malcolm."

There. That's most of it. I try to read his face, but he's as inscrutable as ever.

Just a few more sentences, then. "Not forever," I say. "Not *instead of* your client. Not *in addition to* your client. Just up until I start my life with him. That's all. That's my proposal. And either you're going to give me what I want, or you're not." I settle back against the bench, its wooden slats cold through the thin fabric of my dress.

There's a moment where nothing happens. Then Malcolm drops his indifferent mask and allows himself a soft laugh. He rubs his eyes, shakes his head. He looks different, then; softer, almost. "Do you know what would happen if I said yes, and it ever came out?" he asks.

That isn't a no. I know what would happen. I just don't want to think about it.

"It won't," I assure him.

"I'd be ruined. I know you think you know what that means, but you never will."

I know more than he thinks I do. His brother told me much more than he should have during the hours I spent with him as a punishment for bad behavior with Mistress Fiona. "Gage told me who you were and how you started the agency," I confess.

"Did he tell you how he ended up where he is? It's quite a story."

I'm sure it is, and someday I'd like to hear it, but right now, I'm not going to be blown off course by Malcolm or his dangerous, mysterious brother.

"What do you want?" I ask instead.

Malcolm leans forward, elbows on his knees. All the sounds I was hearing before, other people going about their lives, the world churning on around us—all those distractions melt away, and I'm caught in the green of his eyes, the curl of his mouth. My heart is pounding in my wrists and between my legs. He's wicked enough to dismantle me piece by piece, and gorgeous enough to make me love every second of it.

"You really want to know?" he asks.

"I told you what I wanted. There's no point to that unless you tell me what you want."

"I'm honestly not sure if I'm working with you anymore, but..."

And here he pauses, long enough that the world starts to tug at the edges of my attention. Long enough that I have time to wonder if this is what Malcolm looks like when he's letting someone down easy.

"What I want," he starts again, and then pauses again, and just before I open my mouth to beg him to say it, just say it already, he says, "is to tie you to the headboard by your elbows, spread your legs so wide your cunt's like a bullseye, and fuck you so hard you don't know whether to scream in pain or pleasure."

He stands, his body one long, commanding line, and my throat is dry from want.

"I want to own you so completely you'll suck and fuck anything I put in front of you," he says, crossing the distance between us and placing a hand on my cheek. His skin is so warm against mine. That single point of contact is already too much, and not nearly enough. "I want to send you off to your husband marked with me inside you," he says. His voice is low now, pitched so it falls just between us, rough and urgent. Hundreds of people in this park, and no one knows what we're doing right now. "I never wanted to possess a woman the way I want you, hummingbird."

In the moment, it feels perfectly, unbelievably simple. "Then take me."

"It's dangerous." He pulls his hand away, and my skin goes cold without the warmth of his touch.

"How? If we keep it a secret?" I don't understand how he can say no to this. To us. When it's so clear that we both want the same thing. We'd be explosive together, incendiary. And I'm too caught up in the burn to consider the consequences.

"I don't want you to develop any feelings for me just because I want to own your body. The truth is, I'll never feel anything more for you," he says, his voice as hard as his face.

That stings, but it's for the best, isn't it? My proposal was temporary and limited for a reason. I'm going to marry the Client as soon as the Client is ready to marry me. My body is all I own, at this point, and it's all I can offer anyway. I said it was going to be temporary, and it is. So there's no need to rub it in, but yes, this is what we have to agree to. Malcolm's just being rational.

"You'll never be my husband, Malcolm," I say slowly, emphasizing every word, so he knows I mean it, so he knows I understand the terms of the deal we're making. "No matter what you think. I want a forbidden little fling before I get married. That's all."

A silence falls between us. His gaze is locked in mine but I feel his heat against my nipples, in my throbbing pussy, on my thighs and against my neck.

Fuck. Fuck.

"Open your legs," he says.

Is that a yes? Maybe? Either way, I'm not going to say no.

"Heels on the bench," Malcolm commands. "Skirt over your knees. Let me see what I'm renting."

I kick off my shoes and do as he says, pulling the crotch of my panties aside so he can look at my pulsing center, the core of where I need him.

"Are you wet?" he asks. His voice is rougher than I've ever heard it, still controlled but fraying at the very edges.

I know the answer to his question, but I touch myself anyway, dipping my fingers into my pussy just to watch the hunger deepen on his face when I do it.

"Yes."

He nods and goes back to his bench, leaving a vast, aching gulf of space between us. I'm open and exposed, legs spread, and my skin is broken out with goosebumps that are equal parts fear and need.

"Now," he says. "Show me how a good little slut gets herself off."

It's a relief to touch myself, fill up my emptiness, circle my clit with two fingers. I close my eyes and throw my head back, let myself imagine he's picturing his mouth pressed to the hollow of my throat.

"Eyes on me," Malcolm says, and I snap my gaze back to his. "Keep going, but don't come until I say so. Now, we need to set some ground rules."

The relief quickly turns to torture as my fingers work and my orgasm builds while I try to hold it at bay under Malcolm's impassive gaze.

"One," he begins. "Utter secrecy. Not even your companion. Especially not your father."

I nod my agreement. I would never tell Daddy about this, so that's easy. Jane will be harder but—but whatever. It's worth it.

"Two," he continues. "I own you. I am in charge, and you submit yourself to me. You fuck who I say because *I* tell you to. Three. Obedience. You come when I say, every time I say, but never, ever without permission."

He pauses, watches as my breathing picks up and then smooths out again. I can feel my orgasm collecting behind my eyes, in my toes, my whole body full of it, ready to spill out and over as soon as he says the word.

"Four," he says with a smirk, "Patience. When I call, you show up, and when I don't, you never, ever come after me." There's another pause, and I wonder if that's going to be it when he says, "Five. And this is important. No feelings. Don't get confused, Juliette. I will never love you."

He's going to be in charge for the rest of our time together, but I need to get one last word in here. "Six," I say, voice ragged as I try to keep myself under control. "You let me go at the end." Every time I so much as brush my clit sparks shoot off in my bloodstream, and my cunt is pulsing around fingers, ready, ready, ready to spasm me into heaven. "We cut the cord completely, and I have a happy marriage."

"That won't be an issue." His voice is Master cold, but when he stands, I can feel the heat of his body across the distance between us. God, Malcolm. I can't believe I get to have this from him. Anything at all feels like an impossible luxury, better than anything money can buy—and I would know what that means. What hasn't money bought me?

"You may come," he says, so I do, dissolving myself for him, crying out in pleasure while he watches me go.

2

LYING to Jane is harder than I thought it would be. I shower off the evidence of my orgasm before I go over to her cottage to visit her, but even still I feel like she's going to be able to tell. He never touched me, except for that brief cup of his palm on my cheek, but I feel like I'm covered in his fingerprints, marked in streaks where his eyes whipped across my body.

I love it so much.

"So!" she exclaims the minute I step over the threshold. She's wearing a simple silk dress, and the pale blue color sets off the loveliness of her creamy skin and the crimson sheen of her hair. She looks so beautiful, and so happy for me, and guilt starts to nibble at my contentment. "Tell me everything. What happened?"

I hate to watch her sweet face drop when I say, trying to sound sad but not too sad, "Oh, he didn't show."

"Did you wait? Maybe he was just late?"

"No," I tell her. "I waited. I'm not sure if we're working together anymore, I guess." That much is true, at least. Malcolm didn't seem to know either. I wonder how I can get the Client to tell me without arousing suspicion.

A frown creases Jane's brows. She's been with me through all of my work with Malcolm—all of my life, actually. She's my best and maybe only friend, and I hate disappointing her almost as much as I hate lying to her. But it has to be done. And soon it will be over either way.

"How are you feeling?" she asks.

"Fine," I assure her. "I've learned a lot from him, and if this is how it ends, well, this is how it ends."

She settles onto her couch and I join her, sinking into the soft green velvet. "What does this mean for the wedding, then?" she asks, idly twirling a lock of hair around one finger. I'm glad she's not dwelling on the end of my relationship with Malcolm too much. And why would she? As far as she knows, he's just Master to me. Someone I care for, maybe, someone I want, but not a man I'd betray my husband to have. That would be insane. "Are you done, and it's going to happen sooner? Or maybe they need to find you a new tutor, so it's going to be delayed?" she continues, politely not mentioning the third option, which is that it's off, and I'm going to have to rearrange my expectations for the rest of my life entirely.

"Who knows," I say brightly. There's a tray of cookies on the table, perfect little pecan sandies on a small, filigreed silver platter, and I grab one and take a bite. "These are delicious. Did you make them?"

"This morning," she says. "You're not worried that no one's told you? I know they've kept you in the dark a lot during this period, but I think you deserve more information. This is your future we're talking about."

"Maybe I've just gotten used to it," I say, trying to calibrate my shrug to seem casual without trying too hard.

"I know you," Jane says. "You hate uncertainty. You used to run the algorithm on what Chef was most likely to make for dinner every night. Don't try to tell me you're just relaxing while these men roll the dice with your future."

I don't have an argument against that, and I'm annoyed that Jane knows me too well to just believe my lies. Luckily, I'm saved by a text coming through on my phone—which so few people have the number for, that I know who it is before I see the first word.

The message is as curt as his little white envelopes. *My office,* it says. *4:22 p.m. I've sent you a dress to wear.*

Jane reads it over my shoulder, and I let her—being cagey would only make her more suspicious. Plus, as far as she knows, this is the most normal thing that could be happening. Malcolm refused to do my personal off-hours early morning meeting, but he's calling me in for something more formal, giving me his usual tight, exacting instructions.

"Seems like you're still working with him after all," Jane says, relief clear in her tone.

"I guess so," I say, taking another bite of my cookie. "Glad that's settled."

"Me too," she says. "Let me get you some tea to go with that—they came out a little dry, and they're really much better when you have something to dunk them in."

I ARRIVE at the office exactly on time, wearing the dress Malcolm sent: a pale blue tank dress with a short, swingy skirt. The color matches my eyes, and that gesture feels uncharacteristically sweet, so I'm almost relieved when I walk into his office and see that here, Master is definitely Master. He's standing in front of his desk, suit immaculate, eyes cold, looking every inch like a man who owns the world. He barely has a change of expression when I come in.

The way his gaze skates across my body, cursory and assessing, is blazingly hot. I get the sense that he could tell me anything about my appearance if asked: whether my eyeliner is even the tiniest bit uneven, if my tan has faded since we first met, whether a few stray baby hairs have managed to escape the bottom of my ponytail. The precise shapes of my breasts up to the peaks of my nipples.

The information isn't sentimental. It's necessary. It's as perfunctory as knowing the dimensions of his home and the property it stands on, whether the taps in the kitchen sink work right, which doors stick after it rains. He owns me, and he's here to make sure I'm in good working order.

"The Client has asked me to make sure your anus is prepared so that you don't feel any pain when he takes it," he says, his voice clinical and exacting. He talks about my body like it's nothing more than a piece of meat to him.

"How?" I'm both delighted he's on the case, and terrified of the pain he's preparing me for.

"Elbows on the desk," he replies with a casual friendliness that does little to cover his clinical hardness. "Let's take a look."

I'm trembling with desire as I follow his instructions: my elbows against the unforgiving wood of his desk, back arched, ass nearly exposed by my short little skirt.

He flips the blue fabric up over my hips and tugs my underwear down, thick fingers rough against the delicate lace. Then he uses his hands to part my cheeks so he can see my hole. I try my best to withstand this onslaught of contact and attention, even though everything below my belly button feels like it's gone liquid with need. I even hold my breath to keep from making a sound.

"The plug he sent you to Gage with was very small," Master says, his fingertips exploring between my cheeks now, starting to massage my hole with matter-of-fact firmness. The muscle there flutters, eager, like every part of me, for his attention.

His touch feels so good that it melts my self-control, and I hear myself say, "I disagree."

"Did I ask for your opinion?"

"I'm sorry, I—" but I can't even finish my sentence when he slides a finger inside of me, easy as anything. It feels so much better than that plug did—blood hot and moving, Master at last.

"I didn't." He leans over so his mouth is almost—but not quite—brushing against the shell of my ear, and whispers, "I don't need your opinion about what I own. Do you understand?"

"Yes, sir."

"You're too tight for a slut." He pulls his finger out and then presses it back in again, so that I can feel every ridge of his knuckles sliding past my rim, every tortuous inch of his intrusion into my body. "Anyone fucking your ass would think you weren't begging for it."

"I am."

"No, you're not...unless I tell you to. This ass is mine until I say it isn't. I'm going to train it for cock. I don't want you in too much pain when I let him fuck it."

I know it's against the rules, but still, I turn my head so that I can look at him, so I can see him in this moment. His gaze claims mine, and an electric shock jolts through my body, hot and sharp and clean. We understand each other.

This is what it means to be owned by him.

I turn my face forward again. "Yes, sir."

"Whose ass is this?" He pushes deep inside me.

"Your ass," I say. I can already feel myself opening up for him, this last place breached, my body welcoming him like it does every time. "You own my ass."

"Perfect. You see that envelope next to the phone? Take it, and do what you're told, just like I taught you."

I reach for the envelope, and as soon as its paper touches my hand, he pulls his fingers out of me. I gasp with the loss. He's out of the room before I can even stand up again, but at least I have instructions for what comes next.

3

EVERYTHING IS easy when I'm with Malcolm—Master—whoever he is. I forget the rest of the world when I'm in that man's presence. It's when I'm not that the pressures rush back in, the expectations of my father and family, the risk I'm taking to have this one thing that I need.

So when I get home, I shut myself in my bedroom and put the earpiece the Client gave me for my last lesson in my ear. It's a slim chance, I know, but I kind of miss his reassuring voice, and I want to settle myself again with the sound of it. To remind myself that this terrifying, thrilling thing with Malcolm will end eventually, and I'll go back to my safe, predictable life again. Master Malcolm owns my wings, but the man who's going to marry me is an anchor, keeping me in place.

But even when I tap the earpiece gently, trying to see if I can generate a response, nothing happens. It's dead. I have to wait until the Client decides to contact me to talk to him.

Around 4:00 p.m. Jane comes by with more cookies, these ones perfectly made, but now accompanied by a pitcher of lavender lemonade, because Jane never does anything halfway. We sit in my living room, feet curled underneath us on my couch, and she asks about my meeting: how it went. What I did. What I learned.

I try to walk the line of being honest without being revealing, and it's just as difficult as it was to deceive her this morning. I have so little practice with telling anything less than the unvarnished truth, and Jane knows me so, so well.

"The Client wants Master to help prepare my ass for him," I tell her. "So it was just about that—checking it out. Making an assessment. That kind of thing."

"Checking it out?" Jane raises an eyebrow in disbelief. "With what? Was it hot? Is he going to do it again?"

Usually I would be dying to share these details with her, to dissect everything he did and everything I felt while he did it. And I am, actually, but also, I can't. Who knows what might drop the wrong hint her way? I have to be as discreet and tight-lipped as possible for as long as my secret with Master holds.

"Just used his fingers," I say. "It wasn't a long meeting. I think it was mostly...diagnostic."

It was the polar opposite of diagnostic; it made me feel like my heart was going to beat through my rib cage, like every nerve ending in my body was located around the movement of his finger inside of me. The world reduced to my body and his. And that was just a preliminary exploration. How will I survive it if he ever fucks me for real?

Jane shrugs. "Oh well," she says. "Too bad. It *was* Master, right? You didn't even say who you were working with."

"I basically had my head in my own ass the whole time, so it barely mattered," I say, and Jane laughs, and then I change the subject, hoping she didn't notice that I didn't answer her question.

I GO to the brownstone alone. This address came from the Client, not Master, but it was just as curt as Master's communiques: a street number followed by the word *penthouse*.

The building is located in one of the fanciest neighborhoods in the city, but I can't tell from the outside what it houses: it could be residential or business, or a mix of both. The lobby is plushly gorgeous, wreathed in understated luxury, but it gives me no clues; there's no row of mailboxes or directory to suggest who lives or works here, just burgundy leather and gold-flecked marble and gilt-edged mirrors. I tell the doorman I have an appointment in the penthouse and he calls the elevator for me; inside, there are no buttons for me to push. I stand straight, eyeing my reflection in the mirror, my pink Dior dress and perfect blowout, as it takes me up and up and up.

When I get out, I'm in a penthouse all right, the windows giving me a view of the neighborhood surrounding us, the world reduced to a dollhouse from this height. At first I can't tell what this place is any better than I could downstairs, but after a moment, certain details resolve into focus. That's not a regular jade sculpture sitting in a vitrine—it's a dildo, with a gold-dipped tip and a pearl emerging from its slit. The curtains are billowy raw silk, the palest, sweetest pink, but they're tied away from the windows with leather straps. A discreet business card on a low oak table confirms my suspicions: this is an extremely high-end sex toy shop.

Before I can sleuth any further, a woman bustles in from one of the back rooms. She doesn't match the décor at all—she's middle aged, wearing a yellow pantsuit complimented by oversized plastic glasses frames and bangs that she must have been teased the exact same way since the 80s. Still, she smiles at me and I smile back.

"Juliette," she says. "Rhonda. I've read your file, and I have to say, I'm very impressed with your string of successes."

That's…not exactly how I'd describe the last few months of my life, but if she says so, I'm not gonna argue.

"Thank you," I tell her.

"If you'll just follow me," she says, and leads us into

a smaller room. This one is windowless, carefully lit, with a plush navy carpet underfoot and a small wooden chest of drawers tucked into one corner. There are two chairs, set to face one another, and between them is a table; on top of the table is a dark wooden box that reminds me of the one that Master gave me my pearls in.

Rhonda takes one seat and indicates that I should take the other. She puts her hands on either side of the box and looks at me frankly. "So," she says. "In here we have the beginner kit. Now, given all that you've done, if you wanted to start with something more challenging..." She glances over at the chest of drawers. I'm guessing there're more kits in there.

I always want to be the best student possible, but with the memory of Master's finger in my ass still fresh, I'm not feeling eager to test my limits, especially this early. Probably best not to rush it. "Beginner's fine," I tell her.

"Good," Rhonda says. She doesn't seem to have an opinion on whether I'm up for the challenge or not, and I'm grateful for that. She flips the box open to reveal a series of slender silver rods, each one bigger than the last, outfitted with stoppers and suction cups on the end. "It's fairly self-explanatory," she says, "You start with the smallest, and then..." She lifts up what turns out to be the false bottom of the box to reveal the largest rod, which is so big and thick I'm instantly grateful I didn't demand to start with anything advanced.

If my lessons have taught me anything, it's that going slow is usually a better idea than charging ahead full steam. I'm grateful to know that instinct is going to serve me and my ass well as whatever the hell I'm doing proceeds.

4

At home, I do my best to set the mood: I take a bath that foams with rose-scented bath bombs, and candle-light flickers in the mirrors as I soak and luxuriate. I do a face mask and a hair masque, and when I'm clean and soft and smell like the sweetest summer day, I take the smallest rod from the box, rub it with the lube Rhonda included, and stick it to the wall, about a foot above the floor, exactly as Rhonda instructed.

I've been doing my best to get myself in the mood—playing with my nipples in the bathtub, letting my fingers drift down my belly, across my hips, to the swell of my mound, never quite touching myself where I wanted it most. Thinking of some of the hottest moments of my training: Vlad's fingers grazing the seam of my pussy, Antoine coming on my face for the first time, orgasming with my mouth full of pearls at The Cuffing Club. But faced with the reality of what I'm about to do, all of the atmosphere I've been trying to create swirls out of the room like water down the drain. This just isn't romantic, and it certainly isn't sexy.

It's not supposed to be that way, I know, but… I wanted it to be. And now I'm alone in my bathroom, faced with the fact that, despite my best efforts, I feel more like I'm facing down a medical procedure than preparing myself for sex—let alone good sex—with my future husband.

Well. It is what it is. I've been spoiled so far, having fun with my lessons; this one might be a little more straightforward, a little less of an exploration, but that's fine. The fun part will come later. For now, I just need to do as I've been told. I'm good at patience now. I just have to be patient a little while longer.

I settle a fluffy bathmat under my hands and knees and then back onto the rod, easing my hips towards the wall until it's seated inside of me. The metal is cold and slick, and it doesn't feel bad, but it doesn't feel good, either. Somewhat less interesting than the plug Gage had me wear at his house, and definitely not as arousing as my Master's finger. I still don't understand what the point of having it on the wall is—why couldn't I just play with myself in bed or something?—but I'm not here to question the Client. I'm here to give myself twenty strokes and loosen up the muscles of my asshole, the way Rhonda, all business in her canary pantsuit, told me I should.

Even as I move my hips, easing the rod in and out, it doesn't feel like sex; it feels like being probed. In, out, in, out. The metal warms, but my mind is wandering. It's never a good sign when you're distracted during sex.

Malcolm taught me that.

As if conjured by the thought, my phone vibrates, and when I glance over, I see Malcolm's face on its screen, requesting a video call. I grab the phone off the stool where I left it and put it on the floor in front of me, hovering over it so that when I answer his FaceTime, it looks like I'm sitting astride him, naked, skin sheened lightly with sweat. I do stroke six while his face resolves on the screen, and the sight of him does more for me than any toy ever will. Keeping track of where I'm at during this conversation is going to be… interesting.

"What are you doing?" he asks.

"Getting assfucked by the wall."

"Let me see."

I hold the phone over my shoulder, letting him see how the rod penetrates me and then I slide off of it again.

When I bring him back to where I can see him, his face is tight with irritation. "No," he says. "Wrong. God. The Client…why does he think he can tell me how to do the job he asked for me, *specifically,* to do? This isn't what's supposed to happen. This is… Jesus. No."

I try to keep track of my strokes while he talks—that was, uh, seven, and then eight, and nine, and nine —and wait, that was nine twice, wasn't it. So now ten? Or eleven?

"I'm losing count," I tell him. "I need to do twenty every day. To loosen me up."

"Losing count," he says. He's disgusted with something, and I hope it's not me. "You should be," he continues. "Sex isn't about *counting*. The Client thinks he knows things. He thinks he's qualified to guide you through this. But he doesn't, and he can't see that he doesn't, and he's ruining everything. You need better instruction, better care than this."

I've never seen Malcolm so worked up about anything, and I have to admit it's doing it for me—the flush rising in his cheeks is in direct contrast with the precision and control of his tightly buttoned collar, his perfectly tied tie.

I could probably get off this way, just talking to him, but something is clearly wrong, so I slide off the rod entirely, settling back on my feet and holding the phone out in front of me. Now that I can concentrate on him, I try to catch any details that will tell me about his life—where he is, who he's with, what he's doing—but all I see is his dark suit and a plain white wall behind him. No clues, as usual.

"It's fine," I say. "I don't hate it." But his face stays dark, and panic starts to flutter in my chest. Is he going to tell the Client I complained about his methods? Is he going to make this into a bigger issue than it should be? I was ready to keep doing the lesson. I only complained because...well. Because I wanted Malcolm to make the lesson more fun. "Don't tell him I didn't like it. Please."

Malcolm shakes his head, like the thought never

even occurred to him. "I own that ass, and he needs to treat it better," he says. "It's too late for today, but—when is the next time you're working on it?"

"Tomorrow night, I guess."

"I'll see you then," he says, hanging up before I can get another word in.

5

WHEN I WAKE in the morning, there's an envelope that's been slipped under my front door. The enclosed note gives me a time and a residential address in one of the nicer neighborhoods in town, not far from where I picked up the rods yesterday. It's signed, simply, *M*.

As I'm wondering where he's sending me, and what will happen while I'm there, the earpiece on my bedside table emits a small beep, alerting me that it's on again. I slip it in just in time to hear the Client asking, "How did your first lessons go?"

"Fine," I say. And it did go fine, and that would be all I had to say, but I can't help remembering Malcolm's reaction—the way his eyes blazed cold, and how furious he looked, that the Client was intruding on his territory. That memory makes me wonder how Malcolm would have arranged the lesson if he could have. How much better it could have felt.

"Did you come?" the Client asks.

I debate for a moment between lying and being honest. Does he want me to say that I loved it, that I loved everything he plans for me? Or am I allowed to admit that it felt like a doctor's exam, not a sensual experience?

Well, he just arranged a long vacation so that I could learn how to ask for what I want, so he's going to hear the truth about it. "It wasn't...very sexy," I say.

"Good," he says. He sounds satisfied, almost triumphant. "On our wedding night, when I fuck your ass, it'll be the first time it feels good. Physical penetration is just an act; it doesn't have to mean anything. But that pleasure, that orgasm: those are mine."

So, there is a reason it's so clinical. At least I know that now.

Though the knowledge doesn't make the rest of the training feel any more appealing.

"Tonight, I want you to do your training at The Cuffing Club," the Client continues. "There are people I want to show you off to."

I glow with satisfaction for a moment—I like the idea that I'm worth showing off, and this sounds like it'll be way more fun than taking the second rod into the bathroom for another soulless session—but then I remember Malcolm's note. Shit. I'm supposed to meet up with him at the address he gave. Now I can't go, but, per his rules, I also can't contact him.

"Be at the back door at nine tonight," the Client

says. "I'm sending you something to wear. Bring your toys and have your earpiece in. I'll be listening."

Then the line between us goes dead. That's it.

Shit. Unless I can figure out how to be in two places at once, I'm screwed.

I pick up my phone and open Malcolm's contact. My finger hovers over the call button while I debate what I'm supposed to do next. He really, really did say I shouldn't call him. There were no exceptions. And anyway, he's the one who made a rule. Can he be mad if I follow it?

He might be, but I don't see a way out of this, other than to just…not show with Malcolm tonight, and then explain what happened whenever he contacts me next. That's fine. It's not a breach of contract; in fact, it's the opposite. Disobeying the Client risks revealing our secret, and there are no feelings between us anyway, so he might chafe a little at being disobeyed, but he can't be hurt when I have other things demanding my attention instead of him.

THIS TIME, when I arrive at The Cuffing Club, I don't enter through the front door; my car drops me off at the back entrance, where I'm escorted down a long brick-walled hallway by a disinterested security guard. The pearl-colored silk teddy the Client sent me whispers against my legs as I walk, fluttering around my body and rendering me a series of shadows and shapes, curves and colors. I'm carrying the box of rods with me, its black matte surface resting between my slick palms.

The Client is in my ear the whole time. "You look amazing," he says. "You're going to blow their minds. If I was that guard, I'd try to get a taste of you for myself —but he knows it's not worth his job to even think about it. You're a prize beyond rubies. You were made for cock. My cock."

At the end of the hallway, the guard opens a door and I walk through into a small, luxurious room. It's a private movie theater, set with red velvet seats and polished oak accents, brass sconces gleaming on the walls. It could seat twenty or thirty, I think, but tonight the screen has been rolled up, and only the first two rows are filled.

"Get on stage," the Client instructs in my ear, so I do. "Put the box on the table."

I count six, no, eight men as I walk down the steps and take my place on stage. It's just me and a wooden table up here, in the spotlight.

"Good girl," he murmurs. "You look stunning."

I look out over the seats, and from what I can see, the men in them are just watching me—not talking, not looking at their phones. Just… watching. The spotlight on me makes their features hard to make out, so I can't tell much else about them. They're just broad-shouldered shadows, and their presence unnerves and excites me in equal measure.

"Take off everything but the shoes," the Client instructs.

Okay. No problem. I pull the straps of the teddy off my shoulders, and the fabric slips off my body, pooling gracefully around my feet. I step out of it before unhooking my bra, baring my breasts and their hard nipples to the assembled men. Last of all is my panties. I wonder if they can see how wet I am already.

"Get out the next size rod," the Client says. "Put it up on the floor."

I'm glad I practiced this alone last night so it's easy to do: attaching the suction cup to the floor, and the rod to the suction cup. The audience stays quiet while I do this, and their stoic shadowiness is starting to unnerve me. Are they going to be like this the entire time? It's kind of hot, but it's kind of weird, too.

One of the men in the second row stands up. "Grab your ankles, babycakes," he says. His voice is deep and rough, a basso I feel in my chest.

"Go on," the Client says. "Do what he tells you."

I turn so that my ass is facing the audience and bend at the waist to lay my hands on my ankles like a good ballerina. I'm getting wet already, my body just starting to warm up to the situation, and I know they can see everything.

The guy strides out from the seats and comes to stand behind me. All I can see are his shoes, black leather and shining in the light. What's about to happen? Is he going to fuck me in the ass after all of this?

He doesn't pull his cock out, though. Instead, there's a couple of sounds I can't identify, and then something cool and wet on my ass. Lube, I think, as he spreads it around, barely slipping his fingers inside of my anus, teasing me with pressure and then taking it away. I'm just starting to get into it, my body feeling slick and hot and needy, when he slips those fingers down my crack and then into my cunt.

I can't help it; I let out a surprised little cry. "Oh!"

The Client's tone over the earpiece is serious, severe. "Beg for more."

"Please, sir. Give me more." My voice feels so loud in the quiet room, but it does the trick: the guy reaches between my legs and flicks my clit.

"Jesus," he says. "It's pierced." He tugs on it, and I barely keep my hips from rocking into the pressure. "What a fucking whore, man. Look at her."

His words feel like one of Master's spanks, stinging and arousing, making all of my blood rush to the surface of my skin. He keeps touching me, stroking my pussy, thumbing my clit, rubbing me everywhere, until I let out another needy little cry.

"Beg him to fuck you," the Client says.

"I am a whore. Please fuck me. I need to come." And I do want to. I want to so badly, except I know that—

"Bet you do," the guy says, punctuating his words with an actual slap for good measure. "But nah."

Then he stops touching me entirely, walking away to retake his seat in the audience. They laugh and clap, pleased by his performance, and I can see him waving to them as he goes up the aisle.

I don't know what to do next, but the Client does. "Good," he says. "Now crouch down. Let them all see your cunt." I do, squatting with my legs spread, my wet little pussy more on display than ever, clint ring glinting in the lights. "Perfect, you're a perfect fucking whore," he says. "Now lower yourself onto the rod. Fuck your ass with it. Let them see how well you take it."

I do as he instructs, and the metal is still cold against my skin, but I want to be filled up so badly, and it feels good to have any pressure, anything to clench against and rock back and forth on.

As I start to fuck myself, the audience rises. They filter onto the stage, surrounding me, a looming mass of men. A forest of legs. One by one, they unzip their pants, take their cocks out, and start jerking off, stroking themselves as they watch me move. I can smell them but not taste them, hear them but not feel them, and the friction of that is driving me crazy, along with the pressure in my ass, the orgasm building, building along my spine.

For a while, all I can hear is the panting of my own breath and the slick sounds of fists on cocks, the occasional animal grunt of satisfaction.

"Fuck," one of them says, and then he's coming, spending his load on my collarbones so that it drips down my tits, hot and wet and nasty. The next one aims more carefully for my face, and the next is on my belly, and after that I lose track; it's just the sound of men relieving themselves, groaning in their pleasure, as mine grows more wild and inescapable inside of me.

Eventually they've all come except one man. He's the guy who lubed me, the only one who's touched me directly tonight. He kneels down in front of me and keeps jerking off with one hand while he reaches out to flick my clit with the other. The pressure is delicious, consuming, tinged with pain and exactly what I need, and it feels so good I start to panic.

"Faster," the Client says in my ear. His voice is commanding now, bending me like a bow. "Show me how you'll come when I'm fucking your ass." I up my tempo, my hips snapping up and down, the man's fingers fast on my clit, and here it is. The problem. The insoluble problem I've made for myself.

I promised Malcolm I wouldn't come without his permission. But the Client won't be satisfied if I don't, and I certainly can't explain the rule, and also, I'm not sure I'm going to be able to hold back. My body is turning animal, now, following instinct; I can feel the primal force of need asserting itself, slowly but very, very surely.

Everything is hot and slick and pressure and friction; my ass is full and my clit fucking aches and I'm throbbing everywhere, my whole body pulsing, pulsing, begging for release. I said I was begging earlier, but this is the real thing: utterly desperate, utterly degraded.

"Go ahead, hummingbird," the guy touching my clit

says, so quiet only I can hear it, and my world starts to tear at the seams. "Show us."

I am a hummingbird: tiny heart beating millions of times per minute, body fluttering as I shout and come and shake, tears tracking down my cheeks when I let myself go at last.

6

THAT NIGHT, and the next morning, into the afternoon, I hear nothing from Malcolm. Nothing from his office, either. He must have figured out what was happening, and he must have forgiven me at least a little, since he planted that guy in the audience to give me permission to come. But how did he know? And what does this mean for what happens next between us?

I can barely eat my lunch, even though the Niçoise salad is one of my favorites, and I know Jane is suspicious. So when we're done, I sneak off and call the agency. I can't live with this uncertainty. I have to just… I have to know something. Even if I get in trouble for asking.

The receptionist says Master isn't in, but she transfers me anyway, to the woman I spoke to at the beginning of my training with Antoine. The one who told me he was all right once you understood his methods.

I'm hoping she has more advice or insight or *something* for me today.

"Hello, Ms. Newmont," she says when she picks up. "I'm surprised to hear from you. How can we help?"

Surprised? This isn't the first time I've contacted them and it likely won't be the last, but whatever. She can be shady with me if she wants. "I'm calling for Master," I tell her. I'm hoping that I can tell her some fib that will convince her to help me, but instead she cuts me off, saying, "He only takes calls from students of active clients."

But that—does that mean—I don't understand.

I thank her on autopilot, tell her I get it even though I don't, and get off the phone as quickly as possible. Then I put the earpiece in, but once again, it's silent, and no amount of waiting or tapping or frantic glaring will make the Client's voice appear from it.

Which means that, even though it's also kind of a bad idea, I have to go talk to Daddy.

I FIND him in his office, installed behind his wide wooden desk, sitting in a chair that looks more like a throne than a business accessory. One of my earliest lessons was to never, ever, for any reason, bother my father while he was working, but right now, I don't care. Something is going on that I don't know about, that involves my life and my future, and I need answers urgently. He's had twenty-one years of my cooperation and patience; today, he gets a taste of my temper.

He glances up when I come in and frowns, shakes his head, assuming that I'll come back when it's convenient for him. Instead, I walk deliberately over to one of the chairs facing his desk and take a seat, crossing my legs delicately at the ankles. I will not be put off.

He shakes his head again, and I shake my head back at him.

He's on a call, but he must be muted, because he's typing away on his computer at the same time. After a few minutes, his secretary comes in and hands him a sheaf of papers to sign; she can't hide her puzzled reaction to seeing me here during business hours, but doesn't say anything. Finally, Daddy leans over and unmutes himself on the call. "I have to hop off," he says. "Tell Andre to send me the details as soon as they're finalized."

Then, to me, he says, "It has to wait."

"It can't."

"Juliette, can't you see I'm—" As if to underscore his point, his phone rings again.

"I don't care," I say. "I need to talk to you. Now."

He looks at me. Looks at the ringing phone.

I've never asserted myself with my father like this; I can't remember the last time I disobeyed him, let alone argued that I was right to do it. I feel a small flicker of triumph as he reaches over and silences the call.

"Two minutes," he says. "Today really isn't the day for this."

"It has to be," I tell him. "Because today is the day I called Master's office and found out I'm not a student there anymore. What happened? Was anyone ever going to tell me?"

Any interest he has in appeasing me disappears. "That's none of your business," he says, tone clipped. "You do what I tell you to do, go where I tell you to go, and learn from who I tell you to learn from. In time, you will do those things for your husband, but as of right now, I am in charge of your life and your lessons, and that's all you need to know. You've already delayed me enough for one day. Go."

I gather my courage and stand my ground. "No," I say. "No, that isn't going to work this time. I've done every single thing you've ever said, since I was a baby up until right now. I've done it without question or complaint, and I've done it—all of it—excellently. I've earned a little goodwill, and now I'm spending it, because I want answers. Is Master's agency running the show or not?"

This time, when his secretary peeks her head into the room, presumably to ask why he didn't pick up the phone, he waves her away. "Hold everything until I tell you otherwise," he says, and she scurries off to rearrange his life for him.

Good.

"Your husband decided to take a more active role than your Master weeks ago," he says.

My heart sinks. If Master is just a glorified courier now, there's no excuse for me to see him or talk to him.

Hiding what we're doing will be even more complicated and difficult. But also...why would the Client have done that? Didn't I tell him I was happy with Master, that a change would be difficult for me?

"Oh," is all I say.

"Then I hired him myself," Daddy says.

Jesus. No wonder I'm confused. "What? Why?"

"I'm fine with your future husband running the training the way he wants, but you're still mine," he says. "I'm still responsible for you, and I want you in strong hands. Until you're married and ties are cut, I need you to be watched, and there's no one better. This is his area of expertise, not your husband's. Now, can I get back to work?"

I nod silently and get up, slipping out of his office like a shadow. This changes everything.

Which means I'm not at all sure what's supposed to happen next.

QUESTIONS FOLLOW me as I walk back down the long brick path from the main house to my cottage. It's a beautiful fall day, sunlight crisp through the turning leaves, but all I can focus on is the questions swirling in my head. How can this be happening? Is that how Malcolm knew where I was last night? Did Daddy give him some way to...track me?

Has Malcolm been lying to me?

I let myself into the house and flop down on the

sofa in the living room, feeling more than a little bit like a fainting Victorian heroine from a book. But a fainting Victorian heroine would never have to ask herself what I do now: Is this whole relationship lately —everything that happened in Arcadia, and in the park and his office—just a ruse Malcolm designed so that he could have an excuse to keep tabs on me for Daddy?

I turn over onto my stomach and bury my face in the soft velvet, letting out a groan that no one can hear. Because if there are no feelings, then…so what? Isn't that what we explicitly agreed to? The point was just supposed to be sex, pure and simple.

He said he wanted to own me. Possession isn't a feeling. And maybe all of it was him just saying what he needed to say so that he could do his job.

His job, which matters to him more than anyone or anything ever can or will.

I have no feelings for him, because that was the agreement, and I'm sticking to it. But if I did, they would be tender and bruised.

Being alone with this feeling is intolerable; I'm tormented, and I need someone to take my mind off of it. Before I can overthink it, I get up again and head over to Jane's cottage, hoping she's up for some mindless TV-watching.

When I get there, though, Jane is beaming, and the contrast of her glowing happiness to my thundercloud aura of misery is palpable. She's so excited that she doesn't even notice how dreary I am, just grabs my hands and pulls me into a hug the second I step over the threshold.

"I was just about to call you!" she exclaims. "But you showed up, and that's even more perfect. Oh, Juliette! I have the best news."

She twirls me around the room, and I let her, my body like a ragdoll in her arms. She leans in close and presses her cheek to mine; the satin of her skin is a brief comfort before she whispers, "Bruce asked me to *marry* him," and then pulls away, regarding me with an expression of astonished delight.

I try to arrange my features into a passable smile. I am happy for her. She deserves to have every single thing she's ever wanted.

I want to be happy for my friend. I want it so badly, and I'm in charge of my emotions. If I want to share in her good news, I can. I decide how I feel. It only takes a moment for her delight to wash away my cranky doubt. I am truly happy for her.

"Isn't that wonderful?" she says. "He wants to move off the compound together, and of course I can't until you're married, but I figured, your wedding isn't far off, and then…then our lives will start." She pulls me into another hug, and I bury my face in her shoulder.

"Our lives are finally starting," she says. "I can't believe we're both going to be married women so soon!"

7

JANE'S OPTIMISM RATTLES ME; it's so unsettling to think that we're living in different realities, in certain ways. All she sees is my future laid out before me, as clear as it's ever been, progressing in a straight line. *And it is,* I remind myself. She's not wrong. She just can't see all the details, the one slight detour I'm planning to take before I turn back onto the main road and commit myself to the Client forever.

He calls me before I go to bed that night. I try to tell myself it's a good opportunity to get back on track. And his voice in my ears is still gorgeous, a slick masculine purr that rumbles something low in my belly. "Hello, pet," he says. "You were gorgeous for me last night. Ready for the next size up?"

"Of course," I say automatically, one hand reaching out to root through the box on my nightstand for rod #3. When my fingers close around what I think must be the one, though, I'm surprised—so surprised that I have to look over and check to see that I'm not making a mistake. But I'm not.

Where the difference between rods #1 and #2 wasn't crazy, this feels...massive, like a larger, faster step than I would have expected. I cradle the cold silver in my palms and realize I'm chewing nervously on my lower lip.

"It's...really big," I say stupidly into the Client's silence.

"It is," he says, but he sounds amused with me, and pleased. "After the way you performed last night, I know you'll be able to take it beautifully. You need more than some slender little thing to fill you up, Juliette. You and your hungry little holes."

I let his words shiver across my skin as I go into the bathroom and suction cup the rod to the wall, just like I did with the first one. Then I wait for instructions.

"You might want to play with yourself first," the Client muses. "Suck on your fingers, get them wet. Touch yourself for me. Where no one ever touches you. Where no one will touch you but me."

I suck two fingers into my mouth, getting them slick before I start to probe the tender skin between my cheeks. I'm still a little loose from fucking the rod on stage yesterday, and one goes in easier than I would have thought, knuckle slipping past my rim with no resistance.

"How does it feel?" he asks.

He liked it when I was honest last time. "Okay," I say. "Wet."

"Someday I'll fuck your mouth while you prepare your ass for me," he says. "For today, though, you'll just have to dream about it."

I can't, though. I've never met the Client, and I know if I let myself fantasize, it will be about Master. About his cock in my mouth, in my pussy, splitting me open and filling me up everywhere I need it. And it feels too disloyal to think about him with my future husband in my ears. I already came for him the first time I did this kind of homework assignment. I need to make sure I understand the difference between the sex I crave with Master, and the rest of my life with my husband.

So instead I rock back and forth on my fingers, slipping in the second along with the first, until the Client says, "That's enough. Take the rod now."

"Are you sure? I might need to..."

He laughs. "Juliette," he says. "Don't pretend you don't like it when it hurts a little."

Shame flushes through me, so hot and searing that it's edged with arousal, too.

That deflates, though, when I back on my hands and knees, feeling like a toddler, and slide the rod slowly into my ass.

The first breach is manageable, but it thickens as I go, and I have to pause for a moment to collect myself, to catch my breath.

"How are you doing?" the Client asks. "Maybe next time I'll have you send me a video so I can watch you getting yourself ready for me, like the obedient little slut you are."

"I'm okay," I tell him again. "It's intense."

"Fuck it now, and get used to it." His voice is stern and commanding. "Because once we're married, I'm going to take you whether you're ready or not."

A jolt of adrenaline runs through me at the idea—of him just fucking inside of me, making my body accept him, no matter what my mind has to say about it. It's hot enough to push me the final few inches, so that the rod is fully inside of me, stretching me forcefully. I feel wide open and weirdly full.

"They're only going to get bigger," the Client promises. "So don't slack off, Juliette."

There's a click that tells me he's off the line, but I stay where I am, starting to move slowly, working myself back and forth along the rod until the sensation goes from uncomfortable to intense, but not bad. I'm glad he didn't ask me to touch myself, I think; to pretend this was sexy, instead of what it is, which is... mostly strange. His voice is hot, and so is the way he tells me what to do, but I can't get past how clinical it is, and how detached I feel from the whole experience.

I remember Malcolm telling me that this wasn't the right way to do it; how irritated he seemed by the Client's methods for this part of my sexual education. How would he do it instead, I wonder?

I picture him in the room with me, just watching me do exactly what I'm doing now. But he wouldn't have me fuck the wall, I think. It's embarrassing but it's not... vulnerable enough. He'd have me in bed with my legs spread for him, so he could see my pussy on display, clenching around nothing, wet for him even though he didn't want to use it. Maybe he would lean over and spit between my legs, give me his drool and nothing else. It would be slick inside of me but it wouldn't be enough. I would ask him for more. And maybe he would—

I've picked up a rhythm, I realize, my cunt starting to pulse as I imagine the way Malcolm would teach me this, if he were allowed to. The way he could make me want it, because he can make me want anything, seemingly without even trying.

But the echo of the Client's voice is still in my ears, and so is his earpiece.

I pull off the rod, frowning at the soft squelching sound my body makes when I do it. I have to keep myself together. I can't let the fantasy run away with me.

I stand up, ignoring the pulsing between my legs. Now that I've thought of Master, I want to come, but I don't let myself.

That's enough of this lesson for one night.

I STAY WIRED, though. The arousal I courted earlier burns low and hot in my belly as I twist restlessly in my sheets and try and try and try to fall asleep. So when Malcolm whips the sheets off of me at some pitch-black early morning hour, for a moment, I think I'm dreaming.

When I realize I'm not, I'm pissed. I sit up, trying to smooth my hair and wrangle my temper. "What the fuck, Malcolm?"

He's implacable. "That kind of language is going to get you punished, hummingbird," he says, his eyes raking over my legs, my shoulders, the outlines of my nipples: all of the sleep-warmed skin bared by my tiny chemise and sleep shorts. "I should already punish you for not showing up at my door."

"Yeah—and what was *hummingbird* about? At The Cuffing Club theater?" I spit back. We're not playing his game anymore, and I can dish it just as well as I take it.

"Could you have held it without permission?"

I respond without thinking about it. "What's the difference to you?"

He's done with verbal sparring, though. Instead of answering my question, he shoves me back onto the bed and tugs my legs apart, rough and careless. Then he runs a hand up the inside of my thigh, barely brushing the warm wet of my seam before he pushes my tank top up to expose my tits. He pinches each nipple, watches them get pinker and harder for him, and sticks the fingers of his other hand in my mouth. He tastes like salt, like skin, like victory ribboned in defeat.

My heart is fluttering in my chest, and I remember why he called me Hummingbird in the first place: how

I always feel like I'm going to thrum apart when he puts his hands on me.

He looks down at me seriously, frowning, and pulls his hand out of my mouth. He smacks the side of my ass and says, "Turn over," in a tone that makes me shiver.

"Wait...are you going to—"

"I own you," he says. "What part of 'turn over and show me your ass' don't you understand?"

I get on all fours, expecting a spank—craving it, even—but it doesn't come. He pulls my shorts down around my knees and then doesn't touch me for a few moments. I wait on my hands and knees, ass in the air, feeling exposed and debased.

"I understand," I promise him, but he just pulls my hair in response, yanking my head back so quickly I gasp.

"I'm not sure you do."

"Why don't you remind me, then?" It's dangerous, daring a man like Malcolm, but for once, my provocation gets me what I want. "Fuck some sense into me, maybe."

"Oh, you're getting fucked."

One hand still threaded through my hair, he reaches over to the wooden box on my bedside table, flips it open, and dumps everything out onto the bed next to me. The false bottom tumbles out, the biggest rod coming out with it. He picks it up, and even in his hands, so big and competent, it looks huge. From the way he's looking at it and looking at me, I can tell what he's thinking, and it's not going to happen. I just...I can't. The rod I took earlier tonight already felt massive, and it took me a few minutes to figure out how to relax enough to get it inside. This is way bigger. This is definitely not happening.

"It's too big," I tell him.

"Is it? Open your mouth."

I do, and he slides it in, the metal a cold shock against my heated tongue.

"Is my cock bigger?" he asks.

I nod, because it is, and we both know it—this is very, very big, but his cock is fucking huge.

As if to prove it, he pulls the rod out again, and then presses me flat against the bed. He unzips his pants, pulls himself out and presses his dick inside of my pussy, every single inch so good that all I can do is lie there and take it. This is the first time he's fucked me since he took my virginity in his office, and it's exactly the same and completely different. I know enough now to know that no one else is as big as him. No one else fills me up the way he does. No one else makes my cunt wet and my mouth water quite the way he does when he starts to fuck me, rhythmic and brutal, so that I have to bury my face in the sheets to hide the noises I'm making.

"Every part of your body is built for my cock," he says, riding me still, one hand pressed against my shoulder blade, the other steady and tight on my hip. "Your mouth can take me. Your cunt can take me. So if your ass can take me, it can take this."

Next thing I know, my hips are in the air again, and out of the corner of my eye, I see him pick up the rod from where he dropped it in the sheets.

"My ass can't fit you," I say. I know he's not going to hurt me—I trust him with my life. But also, I'm nervous, my body pumping with adrenaline and desire and nerves.

"Not yet. But it will." He finds the lube that was in the box, and I hear the sound of it, slick behind me, and then two of his fingers are pushing into my hole, just at the edge of what I can take. He works me slowly, in and out, getting me used to the feeling. Are his fingers bigger than the rod was? I can't tell. I'm too overwhelmed. Everything feels hot and shocking and too much and not enough. Why do his hands feel so different than mine did when I opened myself for the Client earlier?

Then Malcolm's cock starts moving inside of my cunt again, the two pressures working in counterpoint to one another, and I can't wonder anything. I start to lose track of what he's doing; all I know is that it feels so fucking good.

"That's right," he says, his voice rough but coaxing, threaded with the barest promise of need. The sound wraps itself around me like silk. "Your ass was made for me." That's when I feel something bigger than his fingers, more solid, slipping inside of my ass, taking their place. "You have it," he promises. "You have this whole thing. Fuck it." I flex and squirm, and he just fucks me harder, his cock still moving slowly inside of me as he pushes the rod in and in and in. "That's right," he says. "That's it."

I'm panting, now, gasping, reeling. All I know is that I'm the object of all of his attention, his instrument. He fucks my pussy and he fucks my ass, and there are universes of sensation inside of my body, stars exploding, galaxies being born, in the pleasure and pain and sheer stunning overwhelm of each gorgeous thrust. It's so much easier to take something this size when I want it—when I need it the way Malcolm makes me need everything he gives me.

"When you take my cock," he says, "it'll be even better."

The silver rod bottoms out, sitting perfectly, and now when he fucks me his hips push it in and out, so that he's in control of every part of me, taking me apart from back to front, inside and out. He reaches around and starts rubbing my clit, fingers strong and sure against that aching little nub, and my body explodes like a bomb: total, certain, without any warning. One minute I'm strung out on what he's doing and the next I'm in the stars somewhere, naked against the black velvet curtain of the sky, sobbing out my release.

When I come back to myself, I expect him to be as in control as always; to be ready to punish me for coming without permission. Instead, when I look over my shoulder, Malcolm has his hips pinned against mine and his eyes closed in bliss; he's coming inside of me, pulsing hot and satisfied, his fingers a brand on my hips, so tight that, even though I know it's a terrible idea, I can't help hoping they'll bruise.

And I feel like someone's set my heart on fire.

EVENTUALLY, he pulls out, and pulls the rod out, leaving me empty and sticky and sated. I lie on my back and look at the ceiling while he goes into the bathroom, and then the kitchen. When he reappears, he has a bottle of sparkling water as well as a small bowl of fresh fruit for me.

I drag myself up to sitting. I should be self-conscious about how I look—my hair is a mess, I'm wearing my chemise still, but no shorts. My body is pink and red and sticky with the aftermath of our sex. But when Malcolm sits down on the edge of the bed and feeds me a plump red raspberry with his fingertips, gentle, careful, I can't bring myself to care.

I drink water and eat the berries, reveling in the quiet of my room, and the feeling of having him in it. Gradually, though, the peace of my orgasm starts to wear off, and my anger starts to simmer again, frustration with him and the situation and how little I understand and how much I might have been lied to roiling under my skin.

"So," I say, once he's given me the last berry in the bowl. "Today I found out you hadn't been my tutor for weeks. And yet, you've been...around. Why didn't you tell me that Daddy hired you?"

He assesses me, much like Daddy did earlier, trying to figure out if he can put me off of this line of questioning. I must look fierce, because he sighs and runs his fingers through his hair. He puts the empty bowl on my bedside table and looks at me. "The Client decided to terminate my hands-on instruction with you," he says. "But your father promptly re-hired me, because he trusts me, and not the Client, to be in charge of your erotic education. As he should."

Hmmm. "So, it's not a betrayal of a client to fuck me anymore?"

Malcolm shakes his head. "It's just as bad," he says. "It would destroy my reputation. People will talk; they won't trust me anymore, not with their wives or girlfriends or mistresses. A sterling reputation for complete and utter professional discretion made my business, and a whiff of scandal could just as easily break it." He sounds calm and dispassionate as he lays all of this out.

His business is his life; if it's at risk, I should take that seriously. But instead, my mind is fixated on the question of what this means about what he said in the garden. Was it true? Does he want to possess me, or was that part of his act?

I know if I bring that up, it will sound like a question about feelings, which will suggest that he has them, or that I care if he does. And he doesn't, and I don't, so I know I absolutely can't.

What I ask instead is, "Does my father know you're fucking me?"

His answer is flat and emphatic. "No."

"Phew. Good. That would be weird."

"It would," he says, just as steady. "Especially if he found out I plan to get inside your precious little ass before the Client does."

I blink at him once, twice, three times, and then he smiles, laughs like what he said was a joke. But the expression doesn't reach his eyes, and he's still intense and focused as he tucks me back into bed, smoothing my hair before he leaves again. Even once he's gone, the sound of those words lingers in the air, and they feel dangerous to me, edged in something tantalizingly, perilously true.

8

THE MANICURIST IS DIPPING my hands into a bowl of sudsy lavender-scented water when my phone buzzes with an incoming text. I have to wait until my cuticles are done soaking before I can pick it up and see what it says, and every second is torture. Will it be the Client? Does he somehow know what I did last night? Or will it be Malcolm—or maybe today he's Master again—telling me what he wants from me next?

I don't know what to feel when I see that the message is from the Client. *I have something perfect planned for tomorrow night,* he says. *It's time for you to try #4.*

I darken the screen and put my hand back where it's supposed to be, watching absently as the manicurist dabs at my nails with practiced precision. After last night, #4 is going to be a cakewalk—but I can't tell him that, of course. As far as he's concerned, the only things

I've ever had in my ass were much smaller, and they were put there by his command, to his specifications.

Another message flashes on the screen. *I still can't stop thinking about how you were so good for me on stage at the club,* he continues. *I got to watch, too, and you were a gorgeous little slut.*

I suppress a shiver as I imagine him finding out what I was doing with Malcolm last night.

You were made for me, the Client says. *You cunt, your ass. They're perfect, and they're mine. I can't wait to watch you come with my cock inside of you. That'll be your wedding gift to me.*

The manicurist is doing a second coat, now, each nail a shimmering pearlescent pink that's as pretty as it is innocent. Guilt starts to curdle in my stomach.

It was one thing when I could tell myself that what I was doing with Malcolm was just fucking: something physical I needed to get out of system, not strictly sanctioned, but not exactly against the rules, either. If I could fuck Jackson Palmer and random men in random board rooms, why not Malcolm? Like the Client said, penetration is just penetration.

After last night, though…it's not the physical acts that would get me in trouble. It's the way I felt about them; how I came with Malcolm's cock in my pussy and the biggest rod in my ass, and now when the Client fucks my ass to orgasm on our wedding night, he won't be the first one who sees how much I love to be filled up that way. The Client is supposed to be in control of my pleasure, but he isn't anymore. Even if I stop seeing

Malcolm right now, I will already have broken his trust, broken the clear and simple rules he set up for me. For us.

But there's nothing I can do about that now.

And in my heart, I know that I wouldn't take it back even if I could.

I'M DISTRACTED for the rest of the manicure and then through my massage, and still while Rowan drives me home from the spa after. There's a question I can't seem to ask myself, and while I swallow it, keeping it just at bay, my brain can't settle, flitting from thought to thought like a hummingbird.

Hummingbird. When I get home, I flip on the TV, but I can't concentrate even enough to watch a show; I try to read a book and the words melt off the page. Finally, I go over to my dresser, where I've been keeping every card Malcolm has given me in a small cedar box. I open it and look at the most recent one, from the appointment I missed in order to go to The Cuffing Club for the Client. It has an address on it, a place I don't recognize, and have never been before.

Before I can stop myself, I go out to the garage and get in the BMW, a sleek black convertible that won't be as noticeable as some of my father's other cars on the streets. I ease out the front gate and onto the road.

I don't know what I'm expecting. It could be a different sex club, or maybe some exclusive restaurant or bar; anything might be hiding behind the bland front doors. *Malcolm might not even be there,* I remind myself.

But when I pull up, it proves to be a house: modern and very neutral, the façade as blank as a page in front of me. I park the car and get out, smoothing my hair and fussing with my pants, which got wrinkled on the drive. My heart is in my throat as I walk up to the front door and ring the bell.

There's a long pause during which I consider fleeing. Running back to the car and back home. Making Jane hide my phone and the keys to every vehicle in the house until I've regained my senses. Forget about the Client—Malcolm told me not to come looking for him, and here I am, breaking the rules. But didn't he break the rules himself, last night?

And anyway, I don't even know he'll be here for sure.

I'm caught by my hesitation, and before I can decide anything, the door swings open, and there he is.

He isn't wearing a full suit, but he's still dressed formally, in a crisp white button-down tucked into navy slacks. He doesn't look surprised to see me. The sun is starting to set behind us, and the world is cast in golden light that catches the impossible green of his eyes and makes the wine in the glass he's holding shimmer. "Juliette," he says, and there's something in his voice that I don't understand.

I'm wet for him anyway.

For a second, I think he's going to send me home;

that even here, Master will replace Malcolm, and I'll be punished with long, cold silence for as long as I can bear it, and then probably longer. Instead, he stands aside and lets me in.

The interior of the house is just as uncluttered as the exterior: everything is beautifully made, and somewhere between handsomely simple and just plain severe. The floor beneath my feet is constructed from wide oak planks; a living room to our left is set with a gray couch and black marble coffee table. There are no magazines on it, no flowers or stray pieces of mail; certainly not the bottle he poured from. I follow Malcolm into the kitchen, where I watch as he presses on a wall panel that slides out to reveal a rack of wineglasses.

"You want one?" he asks.

I don't, actually, but I nod anyway. The kitchen is more of the same: dark wood, black and gray accents, everything carefully put away where it belongs. I don't see a single utensil, not a pot or pan. The oven is visible, but everything else is tucked away, even the refrigerator. Malcolm presses on another panel to reveal a wine rack; he pulls a bottle, opens it, and pours me my own glass. I'm grateful for the sensation of it in my hands: the cold brings me back to myself somewhat.

I follow him to the living room, where I expect we'll sit on the couch and say whatever we're going to say to one another. Instead, just before he reaches the couch, he turns around, still standing, and says, "What are you doing here?"

"I just wanted... I wanted to talk."

"Talk about what?"

I look out the window, into the setting sun. I can feel his presence in the room like a magnet, his body so near, and yet, I'm not allowed to touch it. Not yet, anyway. It's agonizing.

"The Client wants to see me tomorrow night. He told me to bring the next size from the box."

"Charles? Don't worry about him. Just do as you're told, and everything will be all right, hummingbird."

Charles. My mind seizes on the name. Malcolm has never slipped with me before—never told me a single thing before he was good and ready to do it. Why is he being careless now? I didn't even ask for this information, and now I have it, I don't know what to do with it.

He's looking at me like he just gave me a gift, but it doesn't feel like one. Instead, all of my worries from earlier amplify themselves, building and building under my skin. Whatever the name means to me, it's a betrayal of the Client for Malcolm to tell it to me without his permission. And just because he no longer works for the Client doesn't mean we don't both owe him something. Or at least I do, and it's getting harder and harder to remember what that is, much less to hold on to it. Or maybe I'm just making something out of nothing—imagining that this means something, when in fact, Malcolm just said the name because it was a name. In fact, Charles isn't his client anymore.

My mind is whirring faster than ever. *Charles*. Who could he be? Do I know him? It's definitely not Charles

Eastwick—he's 73 and also newly married. Again. Does he have any sons? Young cousins? Who is this man, who bought me a house in the Maldives and insisted I do this training so we'd be on even footing before we even met? Who is this stranger, who is supposed to know everything about me, and yet has no idea of where I am right now, let alone how I feel about it?

It's only been a split second since Malcolm said the name, but when I look back at him, the energy between us has changed. He's ice cold, frozen all over, except for his eyes, which are blazing, almost as if he's trying to melt the icy distance in his face.

"I think," I say slowly, "I've gotten distracted by what we're doing."

He steps forward, closing the distance between us, as silent and smooth as a predator, sleek and dangerous. My whole body responds to his nearness: I can feel myself melting, my nipples straining towards him as the rest of me turns hot and wet and wanting. He takes the wineglass out of my hands without touching me, and puts it down on a small side table.

"What are *we* doing, exactly?" he asks.

It takes everything I have to form sentences. "What *I'm* doing then...I've turned my back on the Client. Charles. We're not even married yet, and I'm lying to him."

He steps closer again. "Are you?"

"I am. And you can say I'm not technically lying, but I feel like I am, and that's all that matters. I have to recommit myself to him....to Charles." All of a sudden,

I'm glad to have a name—it makes him feel more real to me, not just a title but a person. My future husband. My future. "I have to recommit to the promises I've made to him."

Malcolm is close enough to touch me now, and he does, closing one firm hand around my hip. I remember how it felt when he held me there while he fucked into me, and a small, hurt sound escapes my mouth.

"We're just fucking, Juliette," Malcolm says. "Don't take it so hard." He strokes the back of his hand across the peaks of my nipples through my shirt, ghosts his mouth across my throat. He must be able to feel the flutter of my pulse, my heart hammering as I try to hold myself still for him.

"He wants you to experience as much as possible before you marry," Malcolm continues. "Maybe he wants you to experience your own duplicity as well."

I only have another minute of resistance left in me. My pussy is molten between my legs, wet and aching; I want to press up against the hard, flat plane of his body like a dying woman wants water. But I can't let him take me if it's all a game to him. "If that's what's happening—if he hired you to make me feel like a cheater...say it now."

He pulls away, leaving scant inches between us, but it's enough to clear my head just slightly. I could leave.

I'm not going to.

He looks at me, trying to decide if I'm serious, I think. Then he tugs up my shirt and pulls down the lacy cups of my bra, taking my nipples between his fingers, rolling them thoughtfully. "He only cares about your feelings," he says, and then he replaces his hands with his mouth.

"I feel nothing," he murmurs against my skin. My hands come up, helpless, and tangle themselves in his hair. He swipes his tongue against me, one nipple, then the other, before moving downwards, kissing my rib cage, my navel, my belly. One handed, he opens my pants, his mouth hovering just above the newly exposed skin. "Do you feel anything when I do this?"

I'm too undone for lies or half-truths. I don't know what I feel anymore, and this is dangerous, if not for him then definitely for me. I'm about to say so when he pushes me back onto the couch and whips my pants and underwear off, leaving me naked to the soul.

"Spread your legs," he growls. I do, flushing with shame and need as I expose myself. "What do you feel when I look at your cunt?"

He undoes his fly and my mouth waters. There's no coming back from his—how much I want him. How I'll let him do anything to me. Including ruin me.

"Turned on," I say, because it's true, at least.

"I know that. Do you have *feelings*? Because," he says, taking his dick out, already hard for me, the biggest and most beautiful thing I've ever seen, "if you do, we'll stop right now."

I'm sure I do have feelings, but I can't articulate any of them, and right now, getting his gorgeous cock inside of me is more important than any of them.

"I don't," I say, feeling my thighs tremble with the effort of keeping them apart for him. "I don't."

"That's right." He moves towards me, then, pinning me down on the couch and fucking into me in one smooth motion, or bodies joining like they were made to do it. He keeps his face pressed against my neck, his breath hot against my skin, describing what he's doing to me as he takes me apart. "Do you feel anything when I fuck you?" he asks. "When I fill you up with my cock?"

"No," I promise.

"What about when I pull your hair? When I grab your perfect tits?"

"No," I swear. "I feel nothing."

He licks my nipples again, nips at them, each jolt of pain zinging through me and making the pleasure of his cock that much more impossibly good. I feel myself clenching around him, urging him deeper, deeper. I want him to take everything he can get.

"We. Feel. Nothing," he tells me. He reaches between us to thumb at my clit, pulling on the ring and my hair at the same time so that the ache spreads from my scalp to my cunt.

I know my lines. "Nothing," I say.

"We never will. We're just fucking."

Malcolm pinches my clit, hard, and there's nothing to be done about it: I'm coming so hard that the world goes black, shaking and crying out as he fucks me through my orgasm.

In that space, raw and helpless, I know that I was

lying: I am feeling something more than arousal, more than just sheer physical connection when I'm with him. I'm falling for him, and I can't deny it any longer. But between the passion and the dominance, the kindness and cruelty of our encounters, I'm not even sure if I'm falling for Master or Malcolm.

And I shouldn't be falling for either. *Charles,* I remind myself, after Malcolm has come inside of me, when he's walked away to wash up, when I'm lying on the couch still dazed from what he did to me.

I have to recommit myself to Charles. If I can't, all is lost.

9

EVERYTHING in my house reminds me of Malcolm now: the bed where he fucked me, and the bathroom where he let me ride his thigh to orgasm. My dresser holds a box full of his notes and my juggling balls are on the coffee table in the living room, and the faintest hint of his scent is on my pillows when I bury my face in them and inhale.

So in order to recommit myself to Charles, the way I said I would—the way I want to—I know I have to go somewhere else for the day. I tell Jane that I think I saw a mouse in one of the cupboards and ask her to have the cleaning staff give the place a thorough once-over, hoping that the tang of antiseptic will erase my lingering memories. I also tell Jane that I have homework to attend to, so I'll be in one of the guest rooms in the main house all day, and I'm not to be disturbed. She winks at me when I mention *homework,* and I try to smile like I'm excited about what I'm about to do.

I bring the box of rods with me; dutifully, I attach #4 to the wall and slide it carefully inside my ass. It doesn't feel bad; it just doesn't feel like much of anything, after having had the biggest one, plus Malcolm's cock buried in my pussy. I ride it back and forth, twenty strokes. I try to concentrate on the number and the number alone—*one, two, three, four*—but questions keep popping up in my brain. Am I really going to keep up the charade that I need this methodical stretching when I already know I can take the biggest rod?

But that's what he wants, and that's what I'm going to give him. I'm doing everything the right way from now on.

When I finally pull myself off, the earpiece that I left on the bathroom counter beeps to alert me that the Client—Charles—wants to talk. I put it in hastily, hoping the sound of his voice will help put me back on track.

"How are you coming along?" he asks.

"Good," I say. "I just finished with #4."

"Any issues?"

"Nope."

"Good girl. I can't wait to fuck your ass for you, the way it deserves to be fucked."

"I can't wait, either."

"Speaking of which," he says. "We should talk about next steps."

My heart clenches, and I don't know if it's with anxiety or excitement. *It's both,* I tell myself, and it's natural to be anxious about new things and big changes. Getting married is everything I've ever wanted, and I've been waiting a long time now. Of course I'm a little bit nervous. It would be weird if I wasn't.

"I'm planning something for the next size up," he says, his voice a suggestive purr. "Something special for you."

I try to imagine what it might be. Anything would be better than fucking the wall, twenty strokes, clinical and precise. But the idea of another public exhibition doesn't quite sit well with me either. *What do I want,* I ask myself, trying to remember the lessons of Arcadia. Before I can stop myself, I blurt out, "I'll do whatever you want, but…this next time, can it be just us? You and me."

His laugh is rueful but also fond. "Once we see each other, you won't want to finish your training."

That makes sense. But I need something from him—something more than sex games and erotic lessons. "Just with the earpiece then?" I ask. "Like phone sex? But I have an idea to make it really romantic."

There's the edge of a plea in my voice, and I hate that he can hear it. I can't explain it even to myself, why this is the thing I need enough to ask for, but I know that I'm more scared of what happens if I don't ask than what happens if I do.

"Romantic," he says. He sounds like he's considering it.

"Please," I say.

"All right, my pet," he says. "Tell me what you're thinking, and if I like it, we'll do it tonight. Together."

THE PLAN WAS the first thing that popped into my mind, and the first romantic spot I could think of was one of the overlooks up in the hills—near the one Malcolm took me to, though not the same one, of course. I'm a few miles past that particular turnoff, and anyway, it's Saturday; Malcolm's thing was coming here after work. So it's different. It's not like the evening we shared together at all.

It doesn't mean anything, I tell myself as I park the car and put the earpiece in. I slide the driver's seat back so that I have room to stretch my legs out and take #4 from out of its box. The sun is setting over the city again, soft gold light filtering through the air, the sky a riot of blue and pink overhead. The world looks so beautiful and so manageable from up here. The wind has picked up as the day winds down, and it shushes past the windows, a slick rush against the panes.

"Look at you, all alone on a mountaintop," Charles murmurs in my ear. *He's still the Client,* I remind myself. Something as simple and minor as calling him Charles could ruin Malcolm's life as well as mine. "Anything could happen to you, you know. Anyone could see you up here, fucking yourself on a dildo. Then they'd know that you're begging for it."

"I am."

"You're going to get it," he promises. "Spread your legs for me."

He told me not to wear panties, so my cunt is already bare, and already wet; just walking out of the house knowing a breeze could expose me was enough to get me going.

"Skirt around your waist," he continues. "No need to be shy."

The Client talks me through lubing up the rod and sliding it inside of myself, his voice making the actions feel less clinical than they did all those times in the bathroom, at least.

"Imagine how much bigger my dick is," he says. "You're going to cry when I put it in you, and then you're going to cry when I take it out again."

I clench hungrily around the metal inside of me, but there's not enough heft to it; I miss the sensation of Malcolm fucking the biggest one into me, pushing me over the precipice again and again and again.

The reason I'm here is so that I stop thinking about Malcolm.

"Are you wet?" the Client asks.

"Yes."

"Touch yourself for me. Let me hear how my beautiful little slut comes for me."

I start stroking my clit, playing with myself. "Fuck, it feels so good," I moan. "Thank you for letting me have this."

He doesn't respond. Did I say something wrong? I

wait a few seconds, and then try again. "On our wedding night, are you going to fuck me hard?" I ask.

Again, nothing. I ease the rod out of my body, sitting up again, wondering what this means.

In trying to make sure I got lost in the fantasy that the Client was spinning for me, my eyes have fallen shut. But now they pop open, and I see a figure standing on the asphalt in front of me. My heart leaps into my throat.

It's Malcolm, standing in front of the car, hair windswept, shirt unbuttoned at the throat. He's wearing jeans again, and the sight of him unravels something in me.

This, I realize, is what I wanted from Charles: the sense of connection that ripples through me when I see Malcolm, as certain and as strong as an electric current. The way I know him, and the way he knows me.

I open my mouth, as if to ask him something—what could it possibly be? That's when I realize he's staring past me, looking out through the back of the car with rapt attention. He moves to the side, and he's talking as he walks, saying something to someone. Between the wind and the car's windows, I can't hear it.

I turn to see who he's talking to, but all I catch is the back of a man's body as he strides to the other end of the empty parking lot, Malcolm following behind him.

The man is tall and straight-shouldered, wearing an expensive jacket and striding across the asphalt like he's used to being followed. His legs and his strides are long. By the time Malcolm catches up to him, I'm pinned in place, helpless, watching as they have a strange, slow-motion argument that I can't guess at the meaning of.

I'm still frozen when Malcolm looks over the man's shoulder and sees me staring back at him. He frowns and I watch as his mouth shapes a single word, an urgent command: "GO."

I obey him automatically. My hands shake on the steering wheel all the way down the mountain, even after I get home.

10

I STAND, blinking, in the shaft of buttery sunlight that falls across the terra-cotta tiles on my kitchen floor. How can it be morning already? Or maybe it makes sense that it's morning, since last night was so long. I barely slept; instead I shook and cried and went over what happened on the overlook, examining every fragment, until my brain refused to play the tape for me even one more time. Now I'm bleary-eyed and cotton-mouthed, hoping that the coffee I'm brewing will somehow make sense of everything that happened yesterday.

I have so many questions. Who was the other man who Malcolm was fighting with? Was he a peeping Tom, some random guy getting off on me for his own enjoyment? Or was that the mysterious Charles, my future husband, at long last? If it was, he hasn't offered an explanation of what happened—I even went to bed with the earpiece in, but it hasn't beeped once since I got home.

And then there's the question of Malcolm himself. How did he end up there? Was he tailing me for Daddy? Keeping an eye on me for his own reasons?

What were they fighting about? What does this mean?

The La Marzocco on the counter spits a stream of espresso into my cup just as the front door opens, and I hear Jane's voice calling for me. "Juliette? You up?"

"I'm in here," I call back.

She dances into the kitchen, as airy as the sunbeams I'm standing in, and kisses me on the cheek. "Oooh, nice," she says, when she sees what I'm drinking. "Going right for the hard stuff today. Did you have a rough night with the Client?"

I mean to keep lying to her—to keep protecting Malcolm and myself—but I'm too exhausted to hold up the façade, and at the mention of the Client, hot, miserable tears gather in my eyes, which instantly give me away.

"Oh no!" She wraps me in a hug. "What happened?"

The story just comes tumbling out of me. I tell her everything—about meeting up with Malcolm at the park, and agreeing to fuck him with no feelings. About him visiting me the other night, and how much I want him, and how confused I am by everything that's happening. At first she's rapt with attention, but as I get closer to the end of the story—the mystery man on the overlook, Malcolm telling me to *go*—her face has closed down, and she looks almost as upset as I feel.

"Jesus," she says, slumping against the counter. "I can't believe you did all this without telling me."

"I'm sorry," I say, crouching near her, thinking all I did was withhold information.

"I had to! Malcolm's reputation, his business."

"You're ruining everything, Juliette!" And then she bursts into tears of despair and anger. The intensity takes me back a bit. She's too mad for this to be just about the risks I'm taking with my own life. She is pissed enough for two lives.

"How?" I ask. For a moment, her crying distracts me from my own.

"This isn't just about you! *It's my life too*," she says, "You don't even care."

"I do care." I have no idea what she's talking about but I'm sure I care about anything that makes her this upset.

"Do you get what this does to me?" she asks between sobs. "You were supposed to get married, and then I was supposed to get married and move off of this compound with my own husband. To have my own life, for once! Instead, the Client is going to dump you, and I'm going to be stuck here forever, *and* I won't get my bonus, all because *you* couldn't keep your hands off of your hot teacher."

I thought I couldn't feel worse than I already did, but Jane's hurt and sadness compounds my sleeplessness, my anxiety and confusion. I can't believe I was so selfish. I never considered that this might hurt her as much as it could hurt Malcolm or myself. "I'm sorry," I tell her, tasting my own tears as I speak. "I'm sorry, I wasn't thinking. I never meant to hurt you. And I realized last night that I have to stop. I'm going to stop. And if anyone ever finds out, I'll tell Daddy it wasn't your fault. I'll tell everyone—I'm so sorry—I—"

Beep.

We both look over at the earpiece on the counter.

It beeps again.

I pick it up with shaking hands and put it in.

"I want to see you," the Client says, without any introduction.

"See me, as in…"

"In person. I never thought I'd feel this way, but I can't wait another day."

Thank God. "Yes," I say.

"Tonight."

"Absolutely."

Jane is giving me a curious look, so I grab a napkin and a pen out of one of the drawers and scribble *It's the Client. We're meeting!*

She looks so relieved, and I feel terrible all over again. I can't believe I put her through this. I can't believe I'm putting myself through this.

"I'll send you details," Charles says in my ear.

"Okay. But wait—I have to know. At the overlook last night, was that you?"

"I'll explain it to you tonight," he says.

"But—"

I start to protest, but I can hear the line going dead even as the word leaves my mouth. Of course.

Call over.

I take the earpiece out, placing it carefully on the counter. I'm trying to make sense of the tangle of feelings in my chest—hope and relief and exhaustion and uncertainty. This is what I've been waiting for. Tonight, I see my husband's face. Tonight, we forge the connection I've been needing. Tonight, my life goes back to normal.

I take my little cup of espresso like a shot, willing the caffeine to jolt my body back to itself. When I set the cup down, Jane takes it and its saucer out of habit, heading to the sink to wash them. I'm about to tell her not to bother—I'm definitely going to need another one soon—when I hear a knock at the door.

I tell myself it can't be him—it's probably Bruce looking for Jane, or Daddy looking for me, or maybe one of the gardeners coming to ask about the rosebush that we've been talking about replacing with lilacs. He wouldn't come here, not in daylight, just to talk. Why would he? He owes me nothing except his cock, and he's already given me plenty of that.

But when I open the door, Malcolm is standing there, looking like he didn't sleep any better than I did last night.

11

I'M ONLY VAGUELY aware of Jane slipping out the front door after Malcolm walks in. I have no chance to explain that I meant what I said. I'm marrying Charles, not the hot teacher. I send her a silent thank you for her discretion—she can't be happy about this, but she's letting me do it, and it means the world to me.

Then all of my focus is on him.

He's all Malcolm this morning, not a drop of Master in him. He might be wearing the same outfit I saw him in last night, only now he's substantially more rumpled, his jeans creased and his shirt no longer crisp. His hair is messy and there are shadows under his eyes, navy half-moons emphasizing the green of his irises. Somehow, he's more handsome than ever, these rough edges emphasizing the sharp line of his jaw and the irresistible curl of his mouth, the sheer, pure strength of him made clear by the restless movements of his empty hands.

"I have to explain," he says. His voice sounds like it's bearing the effects of being up all night, too.

"You don't," I assure him. "You're working for Daddy. The Client wasn't supposed to know you were there. Was that…the man I saw…was that him, or…" Should I tell him about the call I just had with Charles? I know I should, and I don't want to, but—

"He thinks I'm in love with you," Malcolm says.

For a split second, my mind locks onto the least important thing: so that was my first glimpse of my husband. I only saw him from the back, but he looked like everything I've ever wanted—tall and commanding, certain of himself and how to handle me.

Then I really hear what Malcolm just said.

I may be resisting feelings for Malcolm, and he's definitely not harboring any feelings for me, but Charles thinks differently. How could he be so wrong?

"Yeah, well, you aren't," I say, trying to sound unconcerned. That was the first rule. We both know the deal. I take a seat on the couch, my legs practically giving way underneath me, and Malcolm takes a seat in one of the armchairs, as far from me as possible.

"I'm not," he repeats.

"I know."

"And you have no feelings for me."

The espresso shot is starting to hit my system, making me jittery and unpredictable. "Okay, so did you make this entire trip here to state the obvious?"

Malcolm looks at me for a moment, just looks. His eyes are the clearest things I've ever seen—just pure slick jade green. "I came here," he says, "to resign. I can't work for your father anymore." Before I have time to even process that, he's standing, and I can see Master in the lines of his body, the way he holds himself. "But also," he says, "I came so that we could finish what we started. You, and me."

My throat is so dry all of a sudden. "Finish what?" I ask.

He stalks over to me, tilting my face up with one hand as he sinks to his knees, pressing the hard length of his cock against my leg. Fuck. I get wet for him in one humiliating rush, my pussy pulsing and my cheeks heating and he leans closer and murmurs, "I told you I'd be the first to take your ass, and I'm here now to collect."

I should refuse. I should tell him I'm meeting Charles tonight, and that I'm marrying Charles as soon as he will marry me, and in the meantime, I'm not even thinking about bending the rules, because everything I want and need is right in front of me, ripe as a berry, waiting to be picked.

But he's so close, and so warm, and he smells so good. Last time he fucked me I nearly blacked out from pleasure, and I want to know what his cock feels like inside of my ass. I want to know what it would feel like to let him open me all the way up for him, take everything he wants. Give him everything I have. I'm clenching just thinking about it, my body telling me what its answer is, whether I like it or not.

I try one last time to keep us apart. "I'm seeing

Charles tonight," I say, holding his name out between us like a cross against a vampire, a ward that will protect me from him—and from what I want.

He brushes it aside easily. He rises to his feet, and I come with him, our bodies locking together like magnets, finally clicking into place.

Malcolm says, "Then it has to be now."

Without speaking, we walk into my room, and he shuts the door behind me. Somehow in the process he's transformed fully back into Master again, and his gaze is hot on my skin when he says, "Take off your clothes."

I step out of my sleep shorts, unbuttoning my pajama top with trembling fingers. He's seen me naked plenty of times before, but it feels different now—somehow, I'm painfully aware that we're the only two people in the room. This isn't educational. It isn't for show. It's just me and Malcolm and what we want. It's almost like we mean something to each other, even though I know we don't.

He strokes himself over his pants as he watches, his gaze calculated and considering. The sight of his hardness obliterates any objections I might have had. I need to feel him inside of me one more time.

"Get on the bed," he says. "Hands and knees."

I crawl onto the bed, head down, and wait. He sits down behind me, stroking a hand down the line of my spine, between my cheeks, down to the seam of my cunt.

"Malcolm," I say, but then I don't say anything else, because there's nothing left to say.

"You're wet," he says. "God, you need it so badly."

"I do."

He smacks my ass once and then twice, hard, one for each cheek. I hear him open his pants.

"Get my cock wet for me," he says, moving to the side of the bed so my face is confronted with his massive cock. "It's going to need to be as slick as your pussy if it's going to fit in that tight little asshole."

He doesn't have to ask me twice; I crawl to the edge of the bed and open my mouth. He takes me by the back of the head and impales my face on his cock, pushing hard and deep so I swallow him in a few strokes. He tastes even better than I remember, like salt and skin and sex, and his hands tangle in my hair so tightly that my scalp burns. The weight of him on my tongue and down my throat is so invasive I can barely breathe, and my eyes water as I bob up and down on his length.

"Good girl," he mutters. "Fucking swallow it, just like that." Then he frees one of his hands so that he can play with my ass while I suck him. The angle isn't quite right, and he can't get deep enough to really stretch me; instead, he just touches me enough to make me feel insane, like I want to open up but can't figure out how. I'm in heaven, and I lose track of what I'm supposed to be waiting for, so it's a shock when he pulls my head up and off of him.

"Don't get greedy," he commands.

"I'm sorry."

"You'd better be."

He stands and unbuttons his shirt, revealing the firm planes of his torso and chest. He's thick everywhere, corded with muscle, his skin smooth and tan except for the rough line of hair below his navel. When he's slipped his shirt off his shoulders, he takes his pants off, too, and the sight of him is almost too much for me to take: his enormous cock bobbing, red and wet, between his powerful thighs. He's going to destroy me. I'm going to let him. I've never wanted anything more.

"I should take my time with you," he says. "Take every one of your holes, make you come ten times at least before I put anything in your ass. Make you beg like you've never begged before. Even a whore should pay me something for the pleasure of this cock, don't you think?"

"I'll do anything," I say, and I don't let myself think about how true that is.

"On your back."

He hovers over me, tracing a hand down my body, his skin scribing a burning path from my neck to my collarbones, between my breasts to my clit.

"I'm going to fuck your cunt a little bit before I open you up," he says. "Because this is the first time, and I'm going to need you nice and relaxed when I take your ass. And you know what, Juliette? Just this once, you can come as many times as you want." He tweaks my clit as he says it, and I cry out, convulsing as a wave of pleasure roars through my body.

Then he slides his cock into me, so thick and stunning that my eyes roll back in my head. He fucks me ruthlessly, sucking on my nipples, thumbing my clit, and I've barely finished coming once before a second orgasm sneaks up on me, dismantling me like a plywood shack in a hurricane.

I can't keep track after that; I'm just rolling through my pleasure, giving myself to him. It's like that night at Loki's party with a vibrator tied between my legs, except the pleasure is magnified, because I know exactly who's giving it to me. It's Master, it's Malcolm, with his stern hands and huge dick, his sharp green eyes watching as I come apart at his command.

The next thing I know he's easing his cock out of my pussy while he pushes two fingers into my ass, both of them dripping with my slick.

"That's enough," he says, shifting down to kiss my tits, then my belly. "You can come again when I'm in your ass. Not until then. Not if you want this cock where you need it most. Do you understand?"

"I do."

He doesn't let up on me while he stretches my hole, though, and I'm strung out on sensation. He puts his mouth on my pussy, giving me long, hot licks, and his hands, hot and strong, on my breasts, on my hips, and always pressing deeper and deeper inside of me. After a while he stops touching me to pull away and watch his fingers sliding in and out of me, my body grasping, greedy for more.

"Fucking whore," he spits. I watch helplessly as he lubes up a dick big enough to split me in two. "I'm gonna put my cock in you now. I'm gonna fuck you, and you're going to come without me touching you, and you're never going to forget that I was the first person who fucked your cunt and your ass. I own this orgasm. I own your asshole and your pussy and your mouth, because I. Own. You."

"Yes," I hear myself saying. "Yes, yes, yes, please," as the head of his cock breaches me, so much bigger than his fingers, than the rods, than anything. I only realize I've stopped breathing when he tells me to start again, soothing my sweaty hair away from my face as he keeps pushing in and in and in.

"Perfect," he growls. "Fuck, this is perfect, the way you take it like a whore. Just a little bit more."

"I can't," I gasp, "I can't, I—"

"You can," he says. "You are." And then he's all the way inside of me, scorching, a brand on my body. He's right: I'll never forget this. I'll never get over this.

His thrusts are shallow at first, a rhythmic pulsing that picks up in speed as my body gives around him. He sticks his thumb in my mouth and I suck on it gratefully, glad to have something to fill me up there. I know he told me I could come once he was fucking my ass, but I try to hold off as long as he does. I want to fall off the cliff with him; I want to take him with me when I tumble. To know we're together in this, one last time.

This will never happen again, I tell myself. This is my last chance to feel this, to have this. I keep my eyes open and watch as Malcolm fucks me, our bodies moving in perfect concert. I watch the muscles in his shoulders work, his abs flex as he thrusts into me. I feel the stretch of his cock inside of me, claiming a place no one else has ever touched. My nails score down his back, and at last he leans against my neck and says, "Come for me, hummingbird." So I do, shouting as he shoots inside of me, both of us senseless with pleasure, his body held tight by mine.

12

He slumps against my body afterwards, letting me take all of his weight, just for a moment. I feel the rhythm of his breath, just out of sync with mine: the flex of his rib cage, the movement of his belly. His lips press against my neck, not a kiss, just a touch.

Then he pulls back and pulls out of me, careful as he does it. He doesn't say anything, just gets up and goes into the bathroom. This time, when he parts my legs, he's particularly gentle, swiping at the sticky mess he made of me, cleaning me up. He's intense as he does it, as focused as I've ever seen him, but somehow he still feels far away, like he's taking this all in, but from a carefully-held distance.

I lie still and try to just feel as his fingers whisper across the tender insides of my thighs, my swollen pussy, noting where I'm red from his touch, probing, reminding himself of what he did to me.

The sleep that wouldn't come last night feels possible, now, all of a sudden; my body is heavy and fuzzy and the world starts sliding gently out of focus when I close my eyes.

"I'm going to get you some water," Malcolm says. "Don't fall asleep on me." But he has to coax me awake when he comes back. He holds the glass and has me drink from it like a baby bird, but he won't look at me while he does it. Every touch feels intimately personal and yet strangely absent, and I don't know what to make of it. It feels like a tug-of-war is going on between the Master I first met, a man who broadcasted disinterest and disdain, and the Malcolm I've gotten to know, who's taken care of me like I really am a songbird, delicate between his palms.

I close my eyes again as I settle back onto the pillows, and when he reaches to straighten the blankets that have gotten twisted underneath me, I see something I've been missing for months now. It's so simple, so clear. How did I miss it?

And yet, of course I did. Because I wanted it so much I couldn't possibly let myself think it was real.

"Oh," I say, my voice syrupy with half sleep. "You broke the rules."

"He doesn't have to know."

He's mistaken my meaning. He thinks I'm talking about Charles's rule that he should be the first in my ass. He thinks I'm talking about how he breached his own code of trustworthiness.

Stupid, stupid man. There are more important rules than that.

If he can be obtuse, so can I. I muster the last of my consciousness and sit all the way up. "Do you really not want him to know?" *Tell me,* I think. *Say it, so I don't have to.*

But he isn't going to give in that easily. Of course he won't. That's now how Master or Malcolm plays the game. "Say what you mean, Juliette."

It's now or never. I gather my nerves. *It's ending either way,* I remind myself. And I'm right about this I have to be.

"You broke the rules," I say again, clearer this time. There's no pretending I'm half awake now. I know, and I need him to know that I know this. That as hard as he's tried to hide himself from me, I've seen him. I've seen right through his act. "Between us. You have feelings for me."

He laughs like I'm being ridiculous, but still doesn't meet my eyes. "You and your fucking romantic fantasies."

My resolve wavers. A second ago, I was so sure of myself: sore from his cock, glimmering with the aftershocks of our mutual pleasure, it felt impossible that I didn't know him as thoroughly as he knows me. But I'm stepping all the way out to the edge of a limb here, accusing him of something that would ruin his career —if—and I'm less and less sure every moment—*if* it's true.

But it's not just that. My heart is on the line here, and plenty of my pride, too. What if I try to insist, and he shrugs me off again? I can play this off as a sex-stupid thing to have brought up in the first place. But only if I let it go right now, and never, ever bring it up again.

Maybe it's the force of my orgasm, or just how badly I want it to be true. Or maybe I just say it because, no matter how badly it will hurt to hear whatever he says next, I need some truth more than I need to cling to any delusions after he leaves.

"You can't deny it," I say, willing my voice to stay clear and steady. You've already told me."

Now he does look at me, a fear in his gaze that I've never seen from him before. "I've never said anything that would lead you to think—"

"You have. Not verbally, exactly, but you told me in every other way you could." As I'm saying it, I realize that this isn't the first lie Malcolm has told Charles on my behalf. It might not even be the biggest. After those nights with Mistress Fiona, when I set my own lessons and let a strange man fuck me without anyone's permission, Malcolm covered for me. He did it almost without thinking. Reflexively. Like it had been his instinct all along.

That alone could have broken his reputation and his business, long before he put his cock in my ass and claimed it for himself. He took a risk on my behalf, and I was too naïve to see it for what it was. It's clear to me now.

You don't take that kind of chance for someone who means nothing to you.

But I don't bring it up when I start to list off the rest of the ways he's shown me what he's wanted all along.

"You showed me when you wiped my tears with your handkerchief when Antoine pierced my clit, and when you took me up to the overlook, a place you only ever go by yourself, to be alone," I said, resisting the urge to count on my fingers like a kid. "I saw it on your face while you fucked Trina, but even with your cock in her ass, you were looking at me like you wanted to eat me alive. Even just agreeing to do this—risking your reputation, your business. That's your life, Malcolm. You wagered everything you have so you could possess something my husband won't. You do this for a living. You must have been tempted before. But with me…with me, you gave in."

"I wanted to fuck you, Juliette. Nothing more."

"But you've never wanted to fuck someone the way you wanted to fuck me." I pause, giving him a chance to argue, but he doesn't. "That means something."

"You're mistaken," he scoffs.

"I don't know what it is you're afraid of—"

He stands up, starts to pull his pants on. "I'm not afraid of anything."

But I know, now. I *know*. And I won't let him lie to me—to both of us—anymore. "Why are you so scared of admitting it?" I ask. "It's not Charles. You're not scared of him. It's not your business reputation. It's something else. Something more personal."

"You have a date," he says. "With Charles. The Client. Your husband. You should be getting ready." He finds his shirt on the floor, slides it back on. His hands tremble just slightly on the buttons. His hair is mussed from where I grabbed it, a flush still fading down his chest from how he fucked me until neither of us could stand it any longer. I can't make him stay, but that's fine. I was wrong before. This isn't how anything ends. It's only the beginning between us.

He walks to the door, and it's only then that I speak.

"I'll make you face it," I say, watching his spine stiffen, his shoulders set. He doesn't turn around, but he doesn't keep walking, either. "You forget that I've gotten really good at being patient."

BREAK

I know what I want now.
I know what I *need,* and I don't know if I can live without it.
Or, rather, *who* I need like oxygen.
He needs me too.
I can prove it, I swear, if he'll just give me the chance.
If I can hide what I'm doing from the man who'd forbid it.
I just pray I'm not wrong...

1

Every night, I watch dusk fall and I wait for him. For days, I wear my favorite dresses: sweet, girlish confections of silk and lace, with my favorite lingerie underneath them, all straps and rings, leather and chrome. Then I wear sheer cotton with nothing underneath it, the shadow of my body begging him to slide my skirts up my thighs and slip his cock into me before I have time to say a word. One time, I even strip down naked in the middle of the overlook, my body as bare and vulnerable as I feel. The breeze hardens my nipples, caresses the insides of my thighs. It reminds me with every breath of all the places he's touched me, and how electric it feels every time.

And every night, his car climbs the mountain's curves. He drives a Bugatti most days, with tinted windows and a sleek black exterior that shimmers with power and sex. The tires hug the road no matter how hard he throttles the engine, how his hands move on the gearshift and the wheel.

He slows down just slightly as he passes—long enough to see me, in lace or frills, leather or my own skin—but always wrapped up in desire—just to see that I'm still waiting for him.

Every day, my heart skips a beat when he slows down. Every day, I think today is the day he's going to stop and unlock the door for me to get in. Every day I believe it's going to be the day he drives me away.

But every day, he speeds up again and passes me by, leaving me with a view of his taillights in the twilight and the scents of burnt rubber and scorched hopes.

I can take it. I'm used to acrid stench and bitter rejection. I have been tutored in the arts of patience, and of desire. I am an excellent student of both. I will wait as long as I have to.

Tonight, the sky is vivid pink, the clouds gilt-edged. The air is crisp with fall chill, and I'm wearing something simple: a black wool minidress that nips me in at the waist before flaring out into a pleated skirt. My thigh-high stockings cost almost as much as the dress did, and the seams that run up the back make my legs look miles long. They're hooked to garters, and the chrome of the rings is chilly against my skin.

I stand straight and tall in my black patent heels. The ends of my hair dance at the edges of my vision, soft blonde strands lifted by a light breeze. I feel like a soldier at her post, expecting nothing, but ready for anything.

I hear him before I see him: the growl of his motor, the hush of rubber on pavement. But then a sharper sound cuts the whoosh. My phone chiming in my pocket.

My fiancé's name is on the screen. *Charles.* I press *answer* and hold the phone to my ear, listening as the sound of Malcolm's car gets closer and closer.

"I can't wait anymore," Charles says. "Juliette. The headache you cancelled with before is long gone. It's time for you to stop being afraid. I will see you tonight."

As I draw in a breath to try to respond, Malcolm's car finally rounds the last bend. It's not the Bugatti tonight—he's traded it for a Lamborghini, also black, but even smaller and sleeker, like a bullet in the twilight gloom. I expect the usual—a brief pause, followed by a burst of speed.

Instead, he slows, and keeps slowing.

Of course. The one time I'm on the phone with Charles would be the night Malcolm picks to accept my invitation.

My brain whirrs. "You know I'm devoted to this," I say, letting Charles hear the desperation in my voice. I am genuinely, totally overwhelmed—but he doesn't need to know all the details of what, exactly, is overwhelming me. "You know that. You must. Look what I've gone through already. I can't wait to be with you, but..."

Malcolm's car is turning into the overlook. My heart is hammering in my chest, but I keep my voice steady. “I need some time. I don’t want you to feel like another lesson to me. I want what happens between us to be special. So I think I need a little more of a break to process everything first.”

He takes a long, deep sigh. “As much as I hate it, I completely understand,” he says. “How much time?”

Malcolm parks his Lamborghini next to my BMW and turns it off. I pray Charles won’t hear any of those noises, won’t ask where I am or what I’m doing.

“Not long,” I say. “But listen—I’m losing signal. You’re breaking up.” I’m not sure I’m selling it, but it doesn’t matter; I click to end the call and then turn my phone off, so if he tries me again, it will go straight to voicemail.

I can deal with him later. I need to deal with Malcolm now. Charles is my future, settled and certain, but with Malcolm, I might not have the opportunity to talk to him again if I don’t take it tonight. I’m never sure what a moment between us will be like, and that’s as thrilling as it is maddening.

He gets out of his car, his jaw set and fierce and his movements furiously precise. He’s wearing his usual dark, crisp suit, but his eyes are untamed heat on my skin.

“What are you doing here?” he asks. As if he doesn’t know.

“Waiting for your instructions.”

His tone is curt. “I’m not working with you anymore. Not for Charles. Not for your father. We have nothing to do with each other. You are free.”

I shake my head. He used to be able to fool me with his lies; I took him at face value because I was scared to let myself believe that what I thought might be happening between us was actually happening. But now I know, and my belief in us is as unshakeable as my belief in gravity, in the way the moon pulls the tides. His feelings for me may as well be a physical fact, or a law of nature. And the same goes for what he does to me.

"No," I say. "You'll always be my master."

"That's not how this works."

"For me, that's exactly how it works." My feet are eighteen inches apart; my pussy is deliciously wet for him, my clit pulsing in time with my heartbeat. He taught my body how to want, how to fuck. He made me in the image of his desire. What did he think was going to happen? I want one of his big, firm hands between my legs more than I've ever wanted anything in my life. "I know you have feelings," I say.

"Your behavior is outrageous," he replies. His voice stays cold but his face is marked by fury, which gives him away. "This is a schoolgirl fantasy, Juliette. This is why I never should have agreed to anything unofficial with you. You don't understand the rules of the game." He glances down and straightens a minute wrinkle from his shirt's cuff. "I am a professional," he continues. "I am not a swooning adolescent. And I'm certainly not some pissant with no control. You do not get to walk into my life and believe that you—*you*—know how to break me."

I smile while he talks. I'm barely listening. If he didn't care, he would ignore me; he would never come up here night after night, even just to drive by, and he certainly wouldn't get out of his car to argue with me. I've seen exactly how composed Malcolm can be, how ice-chilled and remote. The sheer fact of his presence here makes a lie of every word of his argument before it even leaves his mouth.

He has an iron will, and he's fighting tooth and nail to impose that will on his disobedient heart.

It's not working.

My lessons with Malcolm were supposed to be about other things: sex and submission, deepthroating and ass-fucking and a million different ways to say *want*, to say *need*. But I learned him, too, during all those months, his tells and his signals, his subtlest signs, and now I can read him like an open book.

All I have to do to get him where I want him is to kneel.

I do it gladly, letting the parking lot's loose gravel bruise my knees and make a thousand tiny rips in my extravagant stockings. He can see straight down the front of my dress, but it's not the bowing of my head or the swell of my cleavage that I'm relying on right now. It's the sheer fact of what I do to him. What we do to each other.

He doesn't say anything. He turns from me, gets in his car, and drives away.

I smile while he does it. I know Malcolm as well as

I've ever known anyone, and in this moment I know that I have him exactly where I want him.

2

THE NEXT MORNING, though, I'm pacing the kitchen in my house, saying too much to Jane. "It's insane," I babble. "It's electric just to stand next to him. When I saw him last night I almost choked on my own tongue, but even if I had, I still would have found a way to suck his dick. The cock on that man—it's so beautiful, and—"

I know she doesn't like hearing this from me; it puts her in a complicated position with my father, who is, after all, her employer. But I don't know what else to do with these feelings. If I keep them bottled up inside of me, I am genuinely worried they'll explode somewhere they shouldn't. Like to a stranger who's massaging my shoulders at the spa, a shopgirl at Agent Provocateur, or one of Daddy's work dinners. Or, worst of all, in a phone call with Charles.

Before Jane can respond, though, I get a text from

my father, which reads simply: *There's someone to see you in my office.*

"I have to go," I say, and Jane waves me off. She's in the middle of making lunch for us, and probably grateful to be spared the distraction of my talking as much as the specifics of what I was saying to her.

I check my outfit in the mirror before I go, and I look presentable enough, I think: I showered and did my makeup this morning, even though I wasn't going anywhere. My hair is pulled into a neat updo, and the Chloe day-dress is navy, so if whoever's in Daddy's office proves to be one of his colleagues, or someone else he needs to impress, I'll look sharp and presentable. Secretly, I hope it's Jacques, one of the stylists I've worked with, with his latest finds from Paris ready for me to try on.

When I arrive, no one is with his secretary. She waves me through the open door. The room is empty. Daddy's big imposing throne of a chair is unoccupied behind is desk, and no one is sitting in the facing armchairs. I wait for a few minutes before I decide to go looking, my heartbeat picking up as I walk into the formal living room, only to find it abandoned, too. When Daddy said his office, I assumed it was something to do with his business, but if whoever this mysterious visitor is wandering the grounds... it might be something else entirely.

Someone who's actually here for me.

I check the galleries next, and the dining room, before popping my head into the kitchen. I'm planning on texting Daddy and then heading back to get the omelets Jane's making us while they're still hot, so I'm surprised to find that, unlike the rest of the echoing house, the kitchen is occupied.

There are two people in there: Ursula, the cook, and the person she's talking to. A man.

I've never seen him before—or I have, I realize, but not really. Last time all I got was a view of the back of his head, the shape of his shoulders and the power of his silhouette. Now I can see his face, and holy sweet goddamn.

He's *beautiful.*

More than beautiful. Movie-star gorgeous, old West handsome, a cowboy and a gentleman and a panty-dropper and a...*fuck.*

Fuck *me,* actually, please.

His smile is molten, a thousand suns at midday in the desert.

"Hello," he says, and the earpiece did not do that voice any kind of justice.

"Charles?"

"Pet," he says. He's melted chocolate and I'm a strawberry, so ripe I could burst.

"I need some dill from the garden," Ursula says. I had briefly forgotten she was in the room. "I'll be right back."

My gaze never wavers from his.

Just. Jesus.

Goddamn.

I try to remember two minutes ago, when my knees

felt like knees and not like gelatin. When my panties weren't soaked with arousal, and my heart wasn't trying to beat its way out of my chest.

"I meant what I said when I called you," Charles says. "I do understand your position. But I also meant it when I said that I can't wait. You're all I think about, Juliette."

He steps closer to me, close enough that I can feel the warmth of his skin, and smell the soft, fresh lemon of his cologne. Underneath that there's a masculine note—pure musk, all alpha—and my throat is perilously dry. Five minutes ago I was absolutely certain that Malcolm was the only person I wanted, but it's hard to withstand Charles's presence, let alone the idea that this man, who could have any woman in the world, wants *me*.

Can't stop thinking about me, in fact.

I've waited so long for this moment, and for a second, I let myself drink him in: his warm, sensuous mouth, and the bright, curious blue of his eyes. The first threads of silver are showing in the tousle of his golden hair, and I can already tell he's going to age like a well-made scotch. His suit fits him perfectly, emphasizing every toned muscle in his body, how powerful he is, and yet how contained.

He's more than I could have asked for, and he's looking at me like, somehow, unaccountably, he feels the same way about me.

But another thing I've learned in the last few months is how to deal with temptation: how to examine my desires and not just give in to them. So as much as I want to just say *yes*, to sink to my knees or offer my throat and find out what he does with me, I stay exactly where I am.

"We're going to spend our lives together..." I say, finally fixing my eyes on the least dangerous part of his body: the Vantablack lapels of his suit. They're immaculate, and I'd bet the fabric would feel perfect curled into my fist. "I'd still like to take things slowly."

I wait for a storm to cross his face, but it never comes. Instead, he gives me another one of those heartbreaking smiles. "Can't blame a guy for trying, can you?" he says. "I won't push you. But before I go..." His gaze dips to my collarbones, my tits and the swollen peaks of my nipples, before finally settling between my legs. "Give me just one taste."

Despite his inability to take no for an answer, I can't help but like him. He's gorgeous, sure, but it's not just that—he wears his power differently than Malcolm, but it's just as present. Instead of feeling tightly wound, utterly controlled, Charles seems like a lion: glorious and beautiful and lazy with his kills. After so long dealing in the abstract and imaginary, *this* is my husband, someone I can know specifically, intimately, and there it is: the feeling I've been waiting for. The one I was looking for when I went up to the outlook. The one I told Jane about.

There's a connection here. Something buzzing and charged in the air between us, the kind of thing you can only feel when you're in the same room as someone, your skin inches from theirs.

So when he closes the distance between us and wraps his arms around me, there's no way I can resist. He dips his head to kiss my neck, my throat, giving me tongue and teeth as I melt into his embrace. His body is hot against mine, broad and firm, and from where his cock presses between my legs it feels like he's big all over.

The next thing I know, he's lifting me onto the counter, shoving my legs apart with his shoulders as he pushes my skirt up my bare legs. I'm not wearing panties, and he seems to approve, if the way he smiles up at me is any indication.

"He told me this was gorgeous," Charles growls, thumbing at my clit ring. "But I had no idea."

I know *he* means Malcolm, and I should be thinking…something…about that, but then Charles puts his mouth on me and the world whites out. He kisses the folds of my pussy, laps at my clit, holding my thighs open as my body starts to shake with need. He seems to know exactly where I want him without me having to say a word, and I hear the trembling little cries coming out of my mouth as if they belong to someone else.

He slips a finger inside of me and I bear down on the pressure, tightening around him like I'll tighten around his cock on our wedding night. He reaches up to pinch my nipple and I keen with surprise and pleasure. No one has ever taken me over so thoroughly before. No one has ever looked so good while he did it, either.

I have my hands in his hair and I'm close to coming when Ursula walks back into the kitchen, carrying a handful of dill and humming to herself. She doesn't make eye contact with me, but she does smile slightly before putting the sprigs on the counter, turning down the heat under the pot on the stove, and leaving again.

Charles tugs on my clit ring once, sharply, and that's what sends me over the edge. I explode against his tongue, letting him taste my orgasm for the first time. He holds my hips in place while it happens, pinning my ass to the cold marble countertop, wringing every last drop of my pleasure out of my body until I'm oversensitive and pleading with him to stop.

"My pet," he murmurs against my thigh. He's beautiful there; he looks like a golden afternoon, a bouquet of flowers, an old-fashioned gentleman washed in sepia tones. Everything my future is supposed to be. "I could eat your pussy for the rest of my life."

3

Two weeks. Two weeks of utter freedom is what I asked Charles for in the kitchen, with my cheeks still flushed from my orgasm; two weeks is what he agreed to, what I now have. Two weeks to do whatever I want with myself, which is an opportunity I've never had before in my life. Fourteen days, and every hour of them belongs to me and me alone.

I'm less than a day into it, though, and all I can think to do with it is give it away. I pace around my room all morning, warring with myself, before I make a decision. Whatever I do has to be done quickly, since this freedom won't last forever, so it's hard to dismiss my anxiety as I text Malcolm, praying he'll answer me. *Can we talk?*

Meeting Charles was better than I ever could have expected, and I can see a future with him now in a way that was impossible when he was just an idea. But I can't move forward with him until I resolve whatever is going on between me and Malcolm. I just need… something. Something more from him. An admission of what I already know: that his feelings for me transcend our business relationship. That I made that igloo of a man melt, at least a little bit. We can't be together, not really, but at least he can acknowledge that he wishes we could.

Except the thing is, he doesn't answer me. I wait an hour, and then two, before I decide to just say it straight out: *I have some time before I have to commit fully to C.*

Again, he doesn't respond.

This is my first day of freedom, and if I'm going to spend it waiting for a text, I can at least surround myself with beauty. Dismissing Rowan, I take the Jaguar to one favorite spots, a small museum that used to be a private home. It has one of my favorite collections, and usually I can get lost between the Giacomettis and the Goyas, but today I keep checking my phone so much that I can see the guards wondering if they need to worry about me, whether I'm going to try to take a photo with flash or stumble into a sculpture.

Even though I came for the art, I can barely even see it. *I want to spend it with you,* I add in another text, in case the previous one wasn't crystal fucking clear.

Nothing. Nothing. More nothing.

So when I leave, I don't head home. Instead, I return to the address Malcolm gave me a few weeks ago. His house. Is this against the rules, still? Are there even rules between us anymore?

How do my previous rules with Charles apply? Am I truly free, or simply not reporting in? I don't really know.

I don't really care. I have to see Malcolm.

The next time I text him, the message reads, *I'm here! On the porch.*

The house is mostly glass in front, big floor-to-ceiling windows that look in on the buttoned-up interior, so I can see as Malcolm walks into the living room and looks at his phone. He doesn't look up, or out at me.

His response, when it comes, is not what I was hoping for. *I have people here.*

It's cute that he thinks that matters. I send, *I don't care.*

He does look out at me, finally, and the feeling of his gaze on me runs through me like lightning. He keeps our eyes locked so that he knows I'm seeing it as he puts his phone down on the table, facedown, so he won't see it light up even if I do text him again. That's fine, though. Now that I'm here, I don't need the intermediary of a screen to get his attention.

A few more people filter into the living room, each of them holding wineglasses and chatting with one another. I can't tell if they're friends or business associates; they're all dressed nicely but not too formally, talking easily with one another. But given what Malcolm does for work, you never know who his colleagues might be. I spot his brother, Gage, and that doesn't help either—I don't know exactly what kind of business Gage runs, but it's Malcolm-adjacent. His brother even helps with particularly troublesome projects, so this get together could still be business or pleasure, or both.

Well, he used Gage just once. For me. Another piece of evidence that what happened between us went beyond his usual practices.

I can hear snippets of their chatter through the window glass, nothing specific, but enough to get a sense of their relaxed laughter. That's fine. They can do whatever they want. I didn't come here for them.

I put down my phone before I start stripping out of my clothes, taking off my blouse and my jeans before stepping out of my bra and panties. It's a little too cold to be naked outside, but I like the way the chill nips at me, making me aware of every inch of my naked body. The idea of everyone in the room noticing me—seeing me putting myself at Master's mercy, ashamed and somehow shameless, turns me on, and the heat of my arousal warms me from the inside out.

I start by touching myself: palming at my breasts, licking my fingers and flicking my clit. No one inside seems to have noticed me yet, and Malcolm has his back to the window, a deliberate gesture I'm sure. So next I crawl onto one of the wicker couches that he has on the porch. It faces the window, so I lean back and spread my legs to give anyone who does care a view.

That's when the first guest spots me—he nudges

his companion, a pretty woman, probably only a couple of years older than me wearing a sexy Gucci dress I recognize from the most recent collection. I let their attention turn me on more as I touch myself, sparks shooting up my spine with every brush of my fingers against my soaking-wet seam.

Most of the party is looking by the time I get up and throw one leg over the couch's arm, pressing my pussy against the wicker bumps. When I start to move, they rub against me in an uneven rhythm, and my breathing gets harsh and unpredictable. I feel wild and filthy, animal. My whole body is pink with desire and satisfaction.

The din in the room has died down a bit, and now I can hear specific voices, specific sentences. They're talking about me.

"This is his job," the first man who saw me is saying. "This is what he does."

"One of his bespoke whores?" Gage says. He squints at me through the glass. "No wait...that one! She's a dirty one, that's for sure. Hey, Malcolm, why not let her in to play?"

I speed up the motions of my hips, hoping to hear Malcolm say yes, to let that tip me over into orgasm. I imagine crawling into the party on my hands and knees, letting him use me as a drinks tray or a fuck toy or whatever he needs.

Instead, though, his voice is empty when he says, "No. The trash stays outside. Caroline, you don't need to see this." He puts an arm around the woman in the Gucci dress and steers her away from the window.

That seems to break the spell; people stay and watch for a little while longer, but they start drifting away after a few minutes. The novelty of me masturbating on the furniture isn't enough to keep them riveted, I guess. But that's fine. I'm not doing this for them. I'm doing this because Malcolm had to turn his back to keep from looking at me, and because I know the vision of me debasing myself for him will set him on fire for me all over again. Because all I have to do is keep getting a reaction out of him, and eventually, that will get me the reaction I want.

The sun is starting to slide west in the sky, and the cold is crawling over me again, numbing my fingertips and toes. *Show's over,* I think. I reach down to pinch my clit and that sends me over the edge; I come with a few stragglers watching, and then I put my clothes on and head back to my car.

It's only after I slam the door behind me that I see the text. *You need to listen. Tomorrow, my office. 9:43 a.m.*

I smile the whole way home.

I couldn't be happier. It's only my first day of freedom, and already, I've managed to score myself a victory.

4

I PRACTICALLY FLOAT into Malcolm's office the next morning. My pussy is wet and wanting but anyone who looked at me would think I was on my way to host a charity dinner. My Louboutins are six inches tall, but my head feels like it's fully in the clouds as I take my place in the chair across from him. Our eyes meet, then I cross my legs primly at the ankle and smiling like the goddamn Mona Lisa as I drop my gaze deferentially.

He waits me out for a good long while—fifteen minutes, maybe twenty, but I wait with equal patience. I never meet his gaze. I am perfectly, exactingly submissive, and it feels as easy as anything. I was born to bow my head to this man. How can he keep denying it?

Finally he says, "You need to stop this."

No, I don't.

I look up at him, finally. He's not Malcolm sitting behind that desk in his double Windsor knotted tie and pocket square. That man is put away while the Master speaks.

"I have feelings for you, and you have feelings for me."

He leans back in his chair and presses a thumb into the center of his palm, as if trying to massage out a knot. *I could do that for you,* I think, but I don't say it, because I don't want to get off track, and besides, he wouldn't let me.

"You don't have feelings for me," he says flatly until he hits the last word. *Me*. That's where I can hear the frustration building in his voice, the thread of his usually impeccable self-control fraying, fraying, threatening to break. Malcolm is infiltrating the Master. "You are free for the first time in your life. You're out to sea and you're terrified. But I'm not your buoy. This is your storm. Own it." He's practically growling by the time he finishes. It is like watching black clouds roll in, lightning sparking over the ocean. Electricity is crackling all over him. *He's* the storm, I think, the one that I would choose if I had any kind of choice.

"I am owning it," I say. "By being here. By telling you what I want."

I stand up.

He stands, too.

I hold perfectly still while he comes around his desk. We face each other, my body pulled taut by the tension between us. His hand circles my neck as he pushes his erection against me, breath hot on my skin. Even through the layers between us, his cock feels like heaven, and I reach for it before he slaps my hands away.

"Disobedient," he says. "From the day I met you." He rucks my skirt up one handed, pulls my panties down so hard I'm pretty sure I hear the fabric rip. Meanwhile, the hand on my throat tightens ever so slightly. "You could have been a perfect whore, but instead, you're just a useless little brat."

I could ask, *then why are you so hard for me*? But I don't, because the answer is obvious.

"You want obedience," I say. "Tell me to open my legs for you."

A derisive little laugh escapes his throat. I expect the command to follow it, but he doesn't need the weakness of words when the power of actions speak louder.

He kicks my feet wide and jams two fingers into my wet cunt.

I let him fingerfuck me, my breath coming in delicious little gasps as the hand on my neck tightens and loosens, tightens and loosens, in time with his thrusts. His gaze is locked with mine, and the only coherent thought I can manage is that I wish he could see what he looks like right now: the fire that's banked and stoked inside of him is undeniable.

I will own my storm, but he has to own the inferno that I've ignited in him, too.

He must be able to tell how close I am, because he takes his hands away just as suddenly as he gave them to me. "Turn around," he says. "Put your whore ass in the air for me. Facedown on my desk. Don't make a single fucking sound."

My panties are around my knees, but I part my legs as best I can, letting him see me spreading for him, desperate no matter what he calls me. He pulls my cheeks apart and spits on my asshole, and for a moment I'm afraid he's going to try to take me without lube, but instead he just spreads it with his fingers and the spit is enough to take the two he pushes inside.

"You think you can manipulate me." He pushes his cock into my cunt, so heavy inside of me that tears rush to my eyes. I take in a silent gasp when he's buried deep, and he smacks my ass once before he starts to move, thrusting in and out. "You don't know what you're doing."

My clit ring rubs against the desk with every movement, and it's an overload of sensation: the fullness of him inside of me, the pleasure of having worked him up so much short-circuiting my senses.

"Don't come," he growls. "Don't you dare come, hummingbird. You don't deserve it."

I don't. I close my eyes and try to lose myself, to float on the knife's edge of my own release without tumbling into it. I have no idea how long he fucks me before he reaches down and wraps his hand around my throat again, harder this time, so tight I start to see stars. If I was insensible before I'm barely conscious now, the world reduced to every gasp of breath I take and the pressure in my pussy, in my ass, the way he surrounds and controls and dominates every one of my senses.

"Of course you love this," he says. "My cock is perfect. I fuck for a living, and I'm the best in the business."

I can't hold on any longer; I don't have enough oxygen to maintain my self-control. I clench around him and come, spasming around his dick so hard that I feel his hips stutter, his orgasm wrenched out of him as helplessly as mine was.

As soon as he's done coming, Malcolm pulls out of me, and I hear him zipping his pants back up. His jizz is sticky between my thighs. I stay spread over the desk, feeling used and pleased about it.

"You do not own me," he says, snapping open a drawer for a wet wipe dispenser, because he's probably got to clean his fingers a few times a day. "Do you understand now that I have no feelings for you, and I never will?"

I let the wreckage he made of my voice with his hands be clear when I say, "I understand that you can't admit yet that you do."

"Do you think you're the first, Juliette? You're hardly the first student that got confused, and you're not even the most delusional. So, let me put this to you plainly. I will never, ever have feelings of love for a woman, and I certainly will never love a whore."

"You don't even believe that."

He doesn't respond to me, so I pick myself up off the desk. My panties are a lost cause—he did rip them

—so I toss them in the trash, $150 of La Perla joining used coffee cups and the wipe he used to disinfect the fingers he had in my ass. I straighten my skirt and my hair. I'm not leaving until he makes me, though. Not until he gives me something else.

"You need to think you have no feelings, but you're afraid it's not true. You're afraid to do what you really want, and you can't deal with the fear. It's crippling you."

"And what's that I'm afraid to do?" He smirks as if this is all a joke. "Love you?"

"To make me your whore."

"Get out."

Ever obedient, I turn to leave with his juices still running down my thigh. I'll walk through the office halls this way to let the entire agency see what he did to me.

I'm half planning what I'll wear when I show up at his house tonight when he clears his throat.

I stop at the door.

"Meet me at the stadium tonight for the game," he says. "Dress like you're accepting an Oscar."

Okay, I think. *That, I can do.*

5

THE GOWN I end up wearing is Valentino, a slinky gold sequin number that looks equal parts Old Hollywood and New Slut with its sky-high leg slit and low-cut front and back. Before I put it on, though, I prepare every inch of my body as if I really was heading to a swanky globally televised event.

I take a long shower, exfoliating myself roughly so that when I smooth lotion on afterwards, it sinks into the softness of my skin and makes me feel like silk all over. I went to Teresa's lingerie boutique yesterday to get a new set, and that goes on next. It's one of the most gorgeous things I've ever owned, almost exactly the same color as my skin, so that I look nearly naked in it. Just the gentle sound of buckles clinking together and satin whispering up my legs making me shiver. I spritz on a layer of Carnal Flower perfume for every layer of clothing I add, making sure the scent of oud and orange blossom dapples my collarbone, breathes across my wrists and wreathes itself through my hair.

I do my own makeup, highlighting and contouring my face to shimmering perfection, but I bring Jane in to do my hair. Things have been a little tense between us since she let Master into my cottage the other day; I had promised her we'd both be married soon, that she'd get to leave and have her own life with Bruce, but as soon as she saw that happen—and how long it took for him to leave again—she knew it wasn't going to be as simple as I'd optimistically made it seem. But she's always done my hair for important events, and there's no one else to help me with this, so I ask her anyway.

"Wow," she says when she sees my dress. "What's all this for?"

"An event," I say, and that isn't, technically, a lie. "I was thinking you could give me one of your special updos to go with it." There's an art to what Jane can do with a little hairspray and two bobby pins, and I'm hoping to flatter her into giving me the style I want without asking any questions I don't know how to answer.

"You want it tight or loose?" she asks. "Is this a chignon event, or are we going for sexy?" There's a prodding to her question, and I choose to ignore it.

"Somewhere in between," I tell her. "I'm not exactly sure who's going to be in the crowd. Mostly, I just need to look glamorous and irresistible."

Whatever her personal misgivings, Jane sets to work, and in twenty minutes, I'm transformed:

perfectly put together, with an updo that can be undone by the wrong shake of my head. It's movie fantasy hair, and I can't stop admiring myself in the mirror while she works. The familiar sensation of her moving around behind me, her fingers on my scalp, the smell of her perfume and mine, and the sight of us in the vanity mirror feels achingly normal, and I let myself pretend for a few moments that everything actually is. That I'm just heading out for a date with my fiancé, and Jane is more than happy to help me get ready.

I try to keep her distracted by asking about how she's doing: I get her to tell me about her most recent date with Bruce, about a new dish Ursula taught her to cook that she's excited to try in her own kitchen, about a dress she's thinking of buying from one of the shops in the city. I think I've gotten away with it, too, until finally, as she's finishing up, she says, "So enough about me. Tell me more about this event tonight. Where are you going?" She spritzes me with a little hairspray and watches as it settles.

"Master invited me to a ballgame," I say, trying not to wince imagining how that sounds to her. *Your future is in my hands, so I thought I'd go to a baseball game with my ex-tutor who I'm not supposed to be seeing at all.* "I think it's an offer of friendship. Maybe professionalism." I can't hide the excitement in my voice, and it's making a lie of my words. She can see right through me.

Jane twists a few last strands away from my face,

examines the effect, and lets them fall again. "I thought you weren't working with him anymore," she says. She sounds ready to be disappointed, but kind of hopeful that she won't be. I am not sure I can let her down, but I'm also pretty sure I will.

"I'm not his *student* anymore. I'll have children with Charles and they're going to need to get married... so..." I shrug without moving my head.

"So Charles will be there?"

Why am I such a terrible liar? Why wasn't telling fibs added to my training? It can't be that much less useful than sucking cock. Deep down, I know that even if I did, lies of omission would still be difficult. Like now—the man I'm taking a break from isn't coming to meet the me and the man I'm obsessed with... but there's simply no way to explain it to Jane that won't upset her.

"No, I don't think he's coming. Does Bruce like baseball?" I make the lamest attempt to change the subject, ever.

"So why did he invite you? Is this a date?"

"I don't think Malcolm even knows how to have a proper date. I mean, can you imagine?"

I make eye contact with her in the mirror, trying to get her in on the joke.

Malcolm bringing flowers to the door. Malcolm making small talk. Malcolm kissing me at the door.

Jane tucks the last pin into place and gives me a final spritz. "But what about Charles?" she asks. "Is he still your fiancé? What does he think about all of this?"

The answer is both too simple and too complicated to give her. I glance at the clock, hoping it will bail me out, and see that I told Rowan to be ready outside five minutes ago. I stand up and grab my purse, pleased that my hair stays where it's supposed to when I move. Jane and I have plenty of time; we can talk about this later. I have to go be with Malcolm now.

"This has nothing to do with him," I assure her. "I gotta go. Thank you!"

And then I'm out the door before she can respond.

I HAD a feeling I'd be a little overdressed, but I wasn't ready for the looks I get as I ascend from Rowan's car, through the bland beige cinderblock hallways, to the skybox where Malcolm directed the security guy to take me. I pass men in Cucinelli T-shirts arm in arm with women in Secret Circus jeans. I am overdressed by a mile. People probably think I'm the team owner's cheap mistress, dolled up like this.

Good. Let them have their opinions.

I'm just glad the slit in my dress allows me to walk quickly enough that I don't fall behind the escort who was waiting for me when I arrived, a thick-necked man in a boxy suit who nonetheless moves like he's on roller skates, murmuring into his earpiece the whole time. I'm also glad I stuck to reasonably high heels—not exactly my Oscar best, but much more practical for navigating around a baseball stadium's concrete concourse than some of the shoes in my collection.

I've been to plenty of skyboxes before, so it's not shocking when we arrive: I know to expect the slick wooden bar and the rows of TVs, the dark, clublike atmosphere. The field below us is bright green, almost neon under the stadium lights, but the people in here are paying more attention to each other, and the waitresses with their trays of golden champagne.

This is the biggest box I've ever been in, though, and definitely the nicest, positioned directly behind home plate. On field, it's the second inning, but already the room is filled with people, mostly men, twenty or thirty of them milling around. They're dressed nicely in slacks and button-downs. Some are wearing suits, and the women are split between sportswear and skirts and dresses. No one is half as dressed up as I am.

I scan the room for Malcolm and find him standing near the front, chatting amiably with a couple. From the set of his shoulders, I can tell he's in Master mode. Next to them is a polished wooden structure, and it takes me a moment to sort out what it is: a stocks, like medieval peasants used to be punished with. There's a resting place for your head and arms, and then a wooden top that closes over you to keep you in place.

My pulse kicks up a few notches. If that's what's in store for me tonight, I can definitely handle it. More than that. I'm almost looking forward to it. If Malcolm thinks he can punish me into not wanting him, he's got another thing coming.

The couple sees me looking, and the woman returns my gaze, giving me a cool once-over and then chuckling to herself. She's wearing a simple shift and flats, looking chic and elegant; next to her, I'm more overdressed than ever.

She turns to Malcolm. "Is this the one you were telling us about?" she asks him lightly, her tone dipped in acid. "The fuckdoll?"

"It is," he says, and then raises his voice so that everyone in the room will hear. "Come here, slut. Turn and face everyone who's fucking you tonight. Let them see if they want you."

I walk over to them on legs that are shaky with adrenaline, turning to look out at the assembled crowd. They can all see the swell of my cleavage, the color in my cheeks, how hard my nipples are in my gown and how easy it will be to slide their hands under its slit.

A man steps forward. He's built like an aging ballplayer, with thick, strong arms and legs, but with a little bit of a gut in the middle. His chin is square and strong, and his eyes are blazing. He squeezes my cheeks until my mouth falls open, and then shoves his fingers down my throat to see if I'll gag.

I don't. I never do. I swallow around him, tasting skin and salt.

He slaps me across the face, once, hard enough to sting. "I'm good to go," he says.

That seems to be the signal, because after he says it, the room descends on me. In just a few moments I lose track of who's touching me—if the hands tugging my gown below my tits belong to the tall blonde with a British accent, or if he's the one shoving a finger in my cunt, laughing when he finds out I'm already wet. There are hands in my hair, between my ass cheeks, touching me like I'm a thoroughbred on an auction block. My skirt's around my waist but my updo is still in place, thank God. Whatever Malcolm's trying to do with this scene, I'm going to prove I'm good enough.

I have no idea how much time has gone by when I hear Malcolm call above the noise of the crowd, "Do we have tonight's toy?"

There's a little conversation between him and the first guy who touched me, plus a couple of other men; they shake hands when they agree, and then Malcolm unlocks the stocks, lifting the top so I can place myself inside of them.

"You can stay or go, right now," he says.

My skirt has fallen to my feet again, but my tits are still out when I walk over to stand in front of him. I keep his gaze locked with mine as I first place my wrists in the wooden divots, and then bend over to lower my neck so that my throat is pressed to its glossy surface. It's lower than I expected, especially with my heels on, and my ass is in the air and on display. Still, I'm not intimidated. This is what he trained me for. I will show him what I've learned.

The field stretches out in front of me; I watch the home team smack a ball over the fence, and the crowd in the bleachers leaps to their feet. They have no idea what's happening just behind them, and the thought gives me goosebumps.

They don't know, but everyone in this room certainly does.

Someone kicks my feet a bit further apart and secures my ankles in a spreader bar before lifting my skirt back up above my hips and pulling my panties down around my ankles.

I've got this. I can take whatever Malcolm wants to give me.

He has someone bring him a chair, which he puts between me and the box's window glass. He sits in it and looks at me. "You are so convinced I love you," he says.

I can only see him when someone spreads my cheeks apart and drops cold lube on it before fucking my ass unceremoniously, jamming his cock inside of me roughly, loosening me with nothing more than the fatness of his dick. The audience cheers. With my face closer to the floor, I can smell the faint scent of stale beer from the thousands of spills that have undoubtedly taken place here over the years.

"You do love me," I tell Malcolm.

"If I loved you, I'd cherish you. I'd worship you. I wouldn't let a guy I don't even know fuck your ass."

"You sure?"

Malcolm laughs coldly. "You think I could love a whore like you?"

The man who's been in my ass pulls out, and there's a brief moment of respite before someone else's cock is in my pussy, fucking me just as hard, smacking my ass while he pumps in and out of me. "That was a nice one," someone says to him. "That dinger George just hit. Think he can keep it up for the rest of the series?"

"We'll be lucky if he can keep it up for the rest of the night. At least this pussy is wet. What kind of whore gets off on being used like this, anyway?"

"Speaking of which, don't hog it."

The third guy is bigger than the first two; he fucks my pussy for a while, sliding in and out idly, before he puts his dick in my ass and I have to swallow a gasp. He's not as big as Malcolm, but it's enough to make my eyes water as he fucks me.

"Hey," I hear him saying to someone behind me. "What do you think? Think Johnson can keep this up, or will Casey bunt one home next?"

"The sac's the next play," a female voice responds coolly. "No question. Unger plays the numbers."

"Want to make it interesting?" He pulls out a little bit to spit on his cock before he pushes it back inside of me.

"Always," the woman responds. "How about, if I'm right, I get to spank the toy until it squeaks."

"And if I am?"

Her response must be a gesture, because he laughs, and agrees. He pulls out and someone else takes his place, but a few pitches later, Casey bunts and they score on a squeeze play. The room erupts in cheers and high fives.

The woman returns. She makes sure I'm empty

while she spanks me, my cunt clenching around nothing as she smacks her open palm against my ass and thighs again and again and again. A group of men cheer her on, reporting to each other as my skin turns pink and then red and then purple with pain.

Malcolm sits in his chair the entire time, watching. He doesn't say anything. He doesn't move to join the train of men and fuck me. He doesn't tell anyone what to do. He just lets them use me however they want me to be used.

I've lost track of who's inside of me when a woman approaches Malcolm, holding a bottle of beer. She's around my age, young and pretty in a pair of white linen shorts and a white tank top. She looks summery and sporty and gorgeous. She's the first person who's dared to talk to him uninvited all night.

"You don't have a drink," she says. "Do you want one?"

"I'm all right." It's the first time he's taken his eyes off of me since he secured the stocks around my neck.

"Is she yours?" the woman asks. Whoever's been fucking me pulls out and comes on my back; I feel his jizz dripping down my crack and between my thighs for a few seconds before another man takes over.

"Come on, really?" Malcolm laughs. "Look at her. But you, darling? Come over here." He reaches out and tucks his fingers into the waistband of her shorts, pulling her closer. She comes towards him easily. "You could be mine."

"You think?" She sounds a little breathless.

"Get these shorts off and let's see."

She starts to tug them down, but it's hard with one hand occupied, so she looks for a place to put her beer down. Malcolm takes it from her and shoves the neck into my mouth. There's not much left in the bottle, but I can taste hops and malt as he smooths his fingers over her hips and tugs her shorts down her long, lithe legs. Her panties come down, too, and he smiles at the sight of her bare cunt in front of him.

He unzips his pants and pulls his cock out, and even though someone's fucking me right now, I feel my mouth water—he really does have the most gorgeous dick I've ever seen. It hurts to watch him guide her onto his lap, easing her down onto him with tender hands and a cascade of praise. "Gorgeous," he murmurs. "Oh, this tight little pussy—does it feel good when I fuck it for you?"

"Yes," she moans, throwing her head back. "Oh my God. Oh my *fucking* God." She trembles as she works herself up and down on him, mouth open from the overload of pleasure she's receiving.

Someone seems to think Malcolm's drinkholder idea was a good one; I feel the icy bottom of a glass on my spine as a new cock takes over for the last one I had inside of me. I've never been fucked this roughly for this long, but it's easier to take then the vibrator was at Gage's party. This guy spanks me while he fucks me, timing every smack for when he's pulled out before plunging back in. Even though my ass is already ringing with the aftershocks of my first spanking, it still feels good, just like it always does when someone gives me a little pain to go with my pleasure.

What doesn't feel good is watching this woman ride Malcolm, bouncing up and down on his cock as he tells her how good she feels, kisses her neck, and massages her clit until she's coming once, and then again, and again. He's fucking her like she's special, like she means something to him, and even though I know she's not, it still stings like crazy.

The woman must feel my gaze on her, because she glances over at me. "She's watching us," she says.

"Who? The drinkholder?" He plucks the bottle out of my mouth and hands it off to someone. "Let her watch. I'll get you a new beer, baby."

The next thing I know, the bottle, slick with my spit, is being shoved into my ass while a dick pounds into my pussy.

"Just a little more," Malcolm is telling the girl in his lap. "Just a little faster, so I can come inside you, fill you up just the way you need it."

She follows his instructions.

I'm close, too: the sensation of having both of my holes filled is starting to light me up, and I want to come, to prove that none of this is too much for me. But I wait, watching Malcolm, waiting for the telltale way his body starts to seize right before he orgasms. I want to memorize the look on his face: the tension that gathers at the corners of his eyes and mouth, his normally impassive face cracking under the strain of his release.

When I see it, I say, "You love me."

There's nothing he can do about it; he shoots inside of her, and I let myself go along with him, my orgasm pulsing through me like a heartbeat. I can vaguely hear the man who's inside of me saying something about it, laughing, maybe, but it doesn't matter. It feels like Malcolm and I are coming together, our bodies in sync even though we haven't touched once all night. I let myself be loud, so that everyone knows that whatever they've done to me, I haven't broken. I won't. I won't let myself.

When I open my eyes again, Malcolm is furious. He shoves the woman off of his lap and stalks off, out of my sight.

When he returns, it's with a wire contraption, which he shoves into my mouth with his fingers. It wraps around my face, the metal cold against my heated cheeks, and holds my mouth open like I'm at the dentist's office. There's no way I can talk now.

That's fine. I said what I needed to say, and we both know perfectly well he heard it.

Malcolm leans in close to make sure I can hear him when he tells me, "Now you'll stop saying that. And stop pretending I mean something to you. I don't. I'm a lie you're telling yourself."

He knows I can't respond, but he can see the look in my eyes and know that I don't agree.

I never will.

He stands up and announces to the crowd, "Her mouth is open for business."

When the first man shoves his dick down my throat, I can taste my own pussy on him. I let him face-fuck me and watch from the corner of my eye as Malcolm finds the woman who was in his lap earlier and draws her in close. He must be apologizing; she looks pouty for a few moments before he says something that makes her laugh. He tucks her hair behind her ears, draws a careful finger down her cheek, the line of her neck, to the hollow of her throat and the tops of her breasts. He cups her pussy over her shorts.

She smiles up at him. It's so tender and intimate that I want to die.

Instead, I focus on keeping my body relaxed, letting these men shove themselves inside of me. Someone plays with the bottle in my ass while he fucks me, and I come again from the pressure, swallowing hard around the cock in my throat as I do it. The guy there slaps my cheeks before he pulls out and spurts on my face. It's hot, and I'm enjoying myself, except when I think about Malcolm.

After a while, though, the customers start to slow down. There's no one in my mouth, so I have a clear view of it when Malcolm gives the woman his number and sends her off. That makes me almost wish there were more men to distract me, to keep me tethered to my body instead of swirling around miserably inside of my own head.

The room gets quieter and quieter, and I'm finally, fully empty, bruised pink and purple and red, skin sticky and covered in sweat and cum, when Malcolm comes over and unlocks the stocks.

I stand up carefully, rolling my wrists and ankles to make sure everything still works.

"Fix yourself before you leave," Malcolm says. His voice is absolutely glacial.

I glance down and realize my tits are still hanging out of my dress. I tuck myself back in, wondering how the dry cleaner will ever get this thing looking right again. I may just put it in the trash and give it up as a lost cause. I wonder if Jane thought to send Rowan back with a change of clothes for me. It would be nice to put on some sweatpants for the ride home.

"Still think you have feelings for me?" Malcolm asks.

I finish with the dress and swipe my wrist across my face, trying to take off the worst of the drying fluids. "Still think you don't?"

For a moment, he seems taken aback, slightly shaking his head. He stares into his drink another moment, then squares his jaw and looks back up at me. For once, I can't read his face, and I have no idea what he's thinking or feeling in this moment.

"Go home, Juliette," he says. "You're not getting any aftercare. Just go home."

There's nothing to do but obey.

6

FEELING like I've just run a marathon, I undress, bathe with my eyes drooping, and salve my own ass half asleep. My body's going to ache tomorrow, but for now, my slumber is deep and dreamless…until Malcolm shows up, tugging my bedcovers down and waking me with a hand on my cheek at some midnight-black hour.

"What time is it?" I ask, still muzzy with sleep.

"Two eleven," he responds. "Take your pajamas off."

"I thought you said—"

"I let myself lose my temper," he says. He sounds as remote as ever, but his hands tell a different story, smoothing their way down my body, outlining my breasts and my hips, brushing against the insides of my thighs, probing carefully at my pussy to see just how tender I am down there after hours of being brutally fucked. "I was angry with you for your disobedience and willfulness, but that doesn't mean I don't have a responsibility to make sure you're okay physically. This isn't about my feelings, Juliette. This is about your safety."

I nod and stretch up into his touch, my bruised-up skin sliding against the silk of my sheets and the warmth of his palms. "Mm-hmm," I say. "Sure. Okay."

"I can tell you showered," he says. "Did you put lotion on afterwards? Something with comfrey, for the pain?"

"I did."

"How's this?" he asks, his fingers drifting down between my cheeks to touch my throbbing hole.

"It's okay." I shift my legs open a little wider, hoping he'll touch me more, slip his fingers inside of me, give me anything, but he doesn't. Instead, he stands.

"Your voice sounds hoarse," he says. "You haven't had enough water. I can't let you get dehydrated."

I refrain from noting that if he hadn't shackled me in a skybox and let ten or fifteen strangers fuck my throat in the first place, after choking me while he fucked me on his desk this morning, I would probably sound a lot better.

He returns with a full carafe and tall glass; he must have plucked a few leaves from the mint plant that Jane keeps on the windowsill, because they're floating on top, making everything taste sharp and cool and perfect.

He sits down on the bed again. I sit up, letting him see my naked body. See what I let those men do to me so I could prove myself to him. I take a long swallow of water and he nods approvingly, his eyes caressing me just as tenderly as his hands were a few minutes ago.

"I'm not going to tell you how to feel," he says. "But I have to tell you that I am not capable of loving you the way you deserve to be loved. I've tried everything to show you, but it's not possible, and I don't know what else you want."

I drink more water. He's right; I was thirsty, and I didn't even realize it. There's no way he can prove that he has no feelings for me, because it isn't true. But I do know what I want from him. What I always want from him. "The way you fucked that woman?" I say.

"She was a plant," he acknowledges. "A setup." For a moment, it seems like he's going to apologize for the duplicity, but he shakes it off to focus on his failure to manipulate me. "Apparently, it didn't work."

"I want you to fuck me like that." I've already come twice tonight, had strangers' cocks shoved in my ass, my pussy, and straight down my throat. But none of that matters to me right now. I always want Malcolm like I'm a virgin, like I've never touched or been touched. The idea of him makes me so hungry. I know he can see it on my face, and in the goosebumps rising on my skin.

"It won't make me able to love you, or anyone," he says.

That's not a no. And I hate the idea that that woman knows him in a way I don't—has felt his tenderness, when all I've ever gotten is his fieriest passion. He's never fucked me in a way I didn't love. I just want to feel what that way feels like, too.

"Do it anyway," I tell him.

He takes the water glass from my hands and puts it on the bedside table carefully. Then he tugs me over so that I'm sitting on his lap, my bare pussy pressed against the fly of his jeans. He bends his head to kiss my neck, my breasts, and I tilt my face up to the ceiling to hide the tears that want to form in my eyes.

I keep my hands busy, unbuttoning the front of his shirt so that I can touch the warmth of his skin; I slip it over his powerful shoulders, and when he smiles up at me, my heart seizes in my chest. He stands easily, holding me in place as he walks us over to press my back against the wall, my legs wrapped around his hips.

"I'd say I should get you ready for me," he murmurs. "So many men fucked you tonight, and you still need my cock to be satisfied. Are you wet for me?"

I bury my face in his shoulder and nod. "I always am."

"Do you want to come before I fuck you?" he asks. "Or while I'm doing it?"

"I want to come on you," I tell him. "With you." I flash for one brief, guilty moment to Charles in the kitchen, the way his mouth felt on me. Then Malcolm is unzipping his fly and pulling his dick out, huge and throbbing against me, and that's the only thing I can focus on.

"Tell me how much you want it," he says.

"Please. Fuck me. Fuck me like you mean it."

"I always mean it," he says, but he's lowering me down so that my feet are on the floor. "You sure you're not too sore for me?"

"No."

He reaches between my legs and strokes me from clit to seam, long and slow and thorough. "I don't know," he says. "You feel a little swollen. I don't want to hurt you."

"Please," I say again, the word broken in half by a ragged sob. I need him so badly. I'll die if he doesn't give me his cock tonight. Every man I fucked earlier was just a rehearsal for this, for what we both needed, which is always each other.

"All right," he says. "You asked for it."

"I need it," I tell him.

The next thing I know, I'm on my back in my bed, and Malcolm is crawling between my legs, pushing into me with aching, torturous slowness.

"Oh," I hear him saying. "Oh yeah, fucking take it. Fuck."

"Yes," I moan, arching into him. "Malcolm, Malcolm—"

"I've got you," he says. "I'm giving it to you."

"Does it feel good?"

He smiles down at me, feral, and thrusts his hips once sharply just to watch me gasp. "Your pussy is perfect," he says. "Almost enough to make up for what a pain in my ass you are. Are you ready to start coming now?"

I nod my head, words deserting me as he reaches

down and starts to rub my clit as he fucks me in earnest. I come easily for him, my hips rolling as I orgasm around his cock, and when I come back to myself, he's still keeping up the same easy rhythm, like he could do this all night.

I want that. I want whatever he'll give me.

He keeps on fucking me until we're both exhausted, our bodies moving in unison, urging each other onwards. I come again and again and again: with his fingers on my clit and in my ass, in my mouth and in my hair. The best feeling, though, is when he presses his face into my shoulder and says, "I can't hold on anymore. You feel too fucking good." And I dig my nails into his back while he presses into me one last time, shooting hot inside of me, both of us finally letting go.

There's a moment, after, when we're lying in bed together, when I really believe it: that this is forever. That this is the rest of my life. He'll say that he's in love with me, and then—I don't know what happens next. I just know that it happens.

But the longer we lie there, silent, the harder it is to hold on to that rosy fantasy. On my back in the dark, I remember who I am, and who I'm with. How he acted the way he just acted with another woman not six hours ago; how I've seen him turn himself on and off at will. The idea that this isn't real—that I was really, really wrong—terrifies me, and once I've thought it, I can't unthink it. Because I understand exactly how deep I'm in now, and I can't go any further without knowing that he's here with me for real.

The idea torments me, and as exhausted as I am, I can't seem to get sleepy. Questions circle me like sharks. *That felt so real. But it looked real with the other girl, earlier. So are you sure? Are you sure enough to keep walking down this path?*

What if you were wrong the whole time?

I close my eyes and try to breathe through it until I can't stand it any longer. I leap up and grab my pajamas off the floor, pulling them on, shaky with adrenaline and confusion and exhaustion.

"Where are you going?" Malcolm asks.

"Was *that* a plant and a setup?" I see him open his mouth to answer me, and realize I don't want to know the answer. This was all a huge mistake. I need time alone to think. To figure out what I've done to myself and my life, and if there's any way to fix my mistakes. "No! Don't tell me. Just go. Get out."

He sits up slowly, and I can see what I did to him—the marks I sucked onto his chest while he fucked me, the flush fading in his cheeks. Tenderness overwhelms me, and I know I have to get out of there before I lose my mind again.

I run out of the house and into the garden, panting. The grass is dew-wet under my bare feet and the night is still and dark all around me.

It's only a few moments later that the door opens and Malcolm steps out, dressed again in jeans and a button-down. His hair is still wrecked, and the sight makes me proud before it makes my stomach turn.

He could walk away without a word. Instead, he heads straight towards me, slowing as he gets closer, giving me time to bolt.

I don't.

When he reaches me, he takes my face in his hands and kisses me, his mouth so careful on mine that I can taste the truth. The honesty. No matter what has ever come out of our lips, or how many lies are in our future, this kiss wipes them all away. He gives me everything with it, and I take it, swallow it, and beg for more.

My kiss demands all of him, and his opens his heart to me.

This kiss is everything.

I was right all along: This is what he feels. What he wants.

Isn't it?

The sound of a shotgun clacking startles us apart, and I see Bruce coming around a corner, aiming down the scope.

"Who's there?" he calls.

I thank every deity I know about that my voice comes out steady when I respond. "Bruce, it's me. Juliette. It's just *us*."

Bruce whips around, but at the sound of my voice he's already relaxing, taking the gun off of his shoulder and engaging the safety.

"Sorry," he says. "I heard a door slamming, and I thought..."

"It's fine," I assure him. "We just had...anyway. This is my tutor, Malcolm. Malcolm, this is Bruce, the estate caretaker. And sometimes security guard."

"A man who knows his way around a plant," he says. "Me too. Nice setup you've got here, Bruce."

He isn't looking at Bruce, though. He's looking at me, and I hear the echo of the question I asked him inside, the one I didn't want answered. It's too dark to see the gardens right now, but that's not the kind of setup or plant Malcolm's talking about.

I was set up. He is the plant. Our kiss was the payoff. And now?

"I'll be on my way, then," Bruce says, calling over his shoulder as he walks away. "Sorry again to bother you."

"It's no bother," Malcolm assures him. "I was just leaving." He glances at me. "I gave you what you wanted."

All the tiny cracks in my heart start to race towards one another, splintering until it collapses, leaving a crater, deep and black, in the center of my chest.

"No," I say, but I don't know what I'm denying. He's stated a fact. "You feel it."

The lips that just kissed me with intoxicating softness tighten with regret.

He shakes his head.

"Goodbye, Juliette."

It's not a *see you later*. It's *bye forever*.

He's given me everything I asked for. He fucked me

like he meant it, he kissed me until I almost collapsed, and now he can walk away. Which means he has nothing left to prove.

He walks into the darkness. I can still taste him on my lips, and feel him between my legs, and I wonder how I'm supposed to survive if this is really the end of us.

7

I SPEND a long time in bed the next morning, hoping that last night was just a dream. Not the sex, of course —the sex was fantastic, the kind of thing wedding night fantasies and really good porn are made of. But the rest of it. The part where Malcolm said *setup,* and then *plant,* and then *goodbye.*

When I finally do rouse myself, it's nearly 11 a.m., and I know I look like a disaster: my hair is a mess from our fucking, and I'm covered in small bruises. The things that didn't hurt last night have decided to make themselves known in the cold light of day, and everything from the soles of my feet to the top of my scalp aches faintly.

So I'm already feeling awful when I see an envelope on the kitchen table with my father's handwriting on the front.

This better be good news, because I'm not playing the dutiful daughter today.

My hands tremble with sleeplessness and adrenaline and rage when I smack the note down on Daddy's desk. My eyes are dry and red, but I can read the words all too well, written in thick black ink on the crisp white paper: I have 24 hours, and then he's cutting me off.

Completely. For good.

"Is this for real?" I ask.

He looks at me severely, and I have a twinge of sympathy for anyone who's ever tried to cross my father. I've never wanted him to look at me like that, and I hope he never does again. He's terrifying when he wants to be, and right now, he wants me out of my mind with fear.

"It is," he says, "for real. What did you expect, Juliette? You think I'm going to keep paying for you to stall and delay the husband I found you? My responsibility is done. Since you're too busy for a husband, I assume you're busy putting a roof over your *own* head."

He takes his glasses off so that there's nothing between us when he asks, "Did you think that I would subsidize your lifestyle forever? A daughter is not a son, Juliette. You are an asset with diminishing returns. You were raised to become another man's wife. To solidify business arrangements and to smooth the way for the men who run the world. If you've decided to carve your own path in life, I can only conclude that you'll be doing it on your own dime."

"What dime?" He wouldn't really leave me with nothing, would he? I've considered what it would like to be on my own—when I thought I failed out of training, and again when Malcolm asked me if I wanted to leave—but deep down I knew I would never do it. I have plenty of skills, but this is the life I was born into, the one that I want. The one where I belong.

Daddy does not look like he's interested in giving me anything more than he already has, though, and the look on his face tells me that if I test him in this moment, I'll live to regret it.

I leave his office in a daze.

Nothing's getting done unless I shake it off.

Okay. Okay. I can be practical.

I know the first thing I need, which is easy: money. Can I sell my shoes? My purses? Or will he keep those, too, give them to his latest mistress or throw them away just because he can? I should start packing now, I think. I should try to squirrel a few of the more valuable things away. He can't possibly know everything I own. He won't miss a pair of Louboutins here or a diamond bracelet there.

I walk to Jane's cottage automatically, the way I always do when I need a sounding board. I'm still in shock, barely processing the news, and I need her to talk me through this, calm me down and set me straight, like she always does.

She isn't home, though. And when I go looking for her, she isn't with Bruce in the toolshed, or tanning by the pool, or in the main kitchen with Ursula—though the cook does give me a wink that makes me blush and distracts me for one tiny second from what's happening right now.

The grounds of my own home start to look menacing to me as I head back to my house, still alone. I remember Bruce with the shotgun last night, how easily he put it down once he heard my voice in the dark. Will I be a stranger here soon? Escorted off the premises with the promise of a bullet pressed against my back or my side? Every gate, every security camera, seems to be trained on me. They used to make me feel safe.

Now they make me feel terrifyingly seen.

In my own cottage, I fling myself onto my bed and finally let myself cry snotty, messy, ugly tears. Everything that's happened in the last few months has been overwhelming, but this is more than that—I feel like I've been smacked in the face by a tidal wave, dragged under and out into the wide-open ocean. Whatever storm Malcolm thought I was in the middle of before, it was nothing compared to what I'm facing now.

And yet despite that—despite everything he's said and done since I told him I knew how he felt about me—when I can breathe well enough to speak, I pick up the phone and call him. I don't even know what I'm planning to tell him, or what I'm hoping he'll tell me. I just know that, in this moment of crisis, I still want to hear his voice.

How did I let myself get in this deep?

He doesn't answer. He doesn't have a voicemail set up, and the phone just rings and rings, the sound increasingly shrill and hollow in my ears.

He doesn't answer the second time I call, after I wash my face, or the third, while I'm rounding up the smallest pieces in my jewelry collection, things I'm fairly certain Daddy will never miss.

It's well after noon, now, and I'm starving and feeling increasingly desperate. How am I supposed to survive this? What does Daddy think I'll do? All I wanted was two weeks to process… or so I said. Does Charles suspect I have feelings for the man hired to train me, feelings he shared with my father?

I pick up the phone again.

This time, I call Charles himself.

He sounds pleased to hear from me. Now that I know how beautiful his voice is in person, I feel a little robbed talking to him on the phone. "To what do I owe the pleasure?" he purrs. "It hasn't been two weeks yet. Did you change your mind?"

My mind whirs. He doesn't sound like the villain I've momentarily built him into. He sounds like exactly who I'm going to marry—a powerful man who's secure enough to request an experienced wife. A man I truly don't have a reason for Daddy to put off. Or a reason for me. "Two weeks until we have sex," I say. "But maybe we could spend a little time together before then? I'd like to get to know you."

There's a brief pause before he answers, during

which all I can do is pray. This is the only card I have left to play, and if I play it wrong—too desperate, too needy, just too confusing—I'm fucked.

Thankfully, Charles says, "How about dinner tonight?"

8

After that, I don't pack. I can't bring myself to do it. Instead, I wrap denial around myself like the softest cashmere scarf and get ready for dinner with my future husband as if it was just that. And he is still my future husband, I remind myself. The future is just a little further off than any of us had planned.

I make sure to prepare myself as carefully as I did for my night with Malcolm at the ballpark: exfoliating knees and elbows, plucking stray eyebrow hairs, and then moisturizing and making myself up to shimmering perfection.

The whole time, though, my hands are trembling, and I can't stop texting Malcolm. *Things have changed. I need help.*

Just call me.

Please, Malcolm.

He gives me silence. Silence. Silence.

And so tonight as the sun goes down, I'm standing

in the driveway in a new dress, a peach silk Halston gown that whips around my ankles in the breeze with a fur stole tickling my bare shoulders. My hair is pulled away from my face, and a simple necklace of rubies and diamonds adorns the hollow of my throat. I added a heavy diamond bracelet around my wrist, too—it's more than I would normally wear to dinner, but I like the added security of having something expensive on me tonight. In case when I come back...

In case I can't come back. Daddy gave me twenty-four hours, but who knows if he'll keep that promise?

The wind picks up, blowing straight through the thin fabric of my dress, and the icy blast chills my bones. It feels like a warning.

I can't be alone out here.

I can't.

And I don't know Charles well enough to have any sense of what he's thinking or feeling about me since our encounter the other day. I want to trust him, but I can't count on him yet. I'm not sure I can count on anyone, which is a terrifying thought.

So I call the only person who might have a read on Malcolm: Gage. He picks up on the third ring, sounding brusque and bothered, but his tone softens slightly when he hears who it is.

"Juliette," he says. "What have you done with my brother now?"

"Nothing," I say. "I actually can't... I can't reach him. I was hoping you knew where he was."

"I don't." Gage pauses to consider his words before

he says, "We had plans this afternoon, actually, and he didn't turn up. But don't worry. Malcolm does this sometimes, disappears on a whim. He's not entirely reliable, unless you're a client of his, which I understand is a burden you no longer suffer. I'm sure he's fine. He is, after all, a big boy." He chuckles at his own joke. "Can I give him a message?"

There's a long, miserable moment where I try to figure out what it's safe to say in front of Gage, both logistically and emotionally. I'm afraid that if I try to speak any of the words I've been thinking and texting, I'll burst into tears, and wreck my careful makeup, get snot on the mink draped over one shoulder. I'm afraid that if I start crying, I'll never be able to stop.

Plus for which, if I tell him the wrong thing, he could ruin my life. Gage would do it with a grin. Some men just want to watch the world burn, and he's definitely one of them.

"What did you *do*?" Gage asks, and now he sounds both scandalized and interested by my silence. Probably more interested.

What did I do? I tried to convince both of us that Malcolm had fallen in love with me. Even thinking it is so humiliating I want to curl up and die, shrivel up like a salted slug. And now that I know the truth—that he probably isn't, that he probably didn't, that I almost certainly humiliated myself and put my entire future in jeopardy for no reason—I'm still left hoping he'll respect whatever it is we do have enough to at least stay my Master. To take me in, and let me live in the fantasy world he made me, or that I've been making for myself. Either way, it's still the only thing I can bring myself to truly want. I don't know what that means for me, or for me and Charles. I just know that it's the thing that makes the most sense to me in this moment.

"It's complicated," is all I can muster for Gage. "Can you just please tell him to call me?"

Gage sighs theatrically. "It's always complicated with you, isn't it?"

He ends the call, and I slip my phone back into my bag regretfully, thinking of the chess game I lost on Arcadia. That I lost on purpose, playing for something I thought was bigger than myself. Now I've made a series of wild, desperate moves, and I'm backed into a corner, with nowhere to go. I imagine Malcolm, eyes impassive, his cock in some other girl's mouth, his hands threaded through her hair, saying to me: *Checkmate.*

It's possible that by the end of the night, all I'll have is this fur and my jewels. A couple of yards of peach silk, an expensive education, a PhD in fucking, no one to rely on, and absolutely nowhere to go.

Charles's car pulls into the driveway, an elegant black Bentley soft top convertible—though I'm grateful for my hair's sake that he's got the top up tonight. The passenger side door glides open, and I slide myself into the car's luxe interior, grateful for the way it shuts out the rest of the world, enclosing me in a temporary oyster shell of luxury.

Charles looks just as handsome here as he did in the

kitchen, clad in a navy suit that sets off the blue of his eyes and a gorgeous caramel tan. I note the flex of his hand on the steering wheel's leather, the precise way his shirt's cuff reveals the bones of his wrist and the heavy platinum of his Patek watch. A warm thrill rolls itself quietly through my body. If I had never met Malcolm, I would want this man to distraction.

As it is, I'm frankly still pretty distracted.

"I'm glad you wanted to see me," he says. He reaches that hand over and puts it on my thigh. My legs part impulsively, automatically, shifting to make room for him, but he doesn't take the invitation. Instead, he takes my hand in his, lacing our fingers together, and kisses them. "You look stunning."

"Thank you." A blush heats my cheeks, and I know he can see my nipples hardening through my dress. I purposely didn't wear a bra, and even though I've done much more debased things in front of many more people, I still feel a little shocked at my own brashness. It's one thing to look like a slut at a sex club; it's another to show up half-naked to a public dinner with the fiancé you barely know. But I like it, and from what I've been tutored in, I can only guess that Charles does, too.

"That dress," he says. "I like your style." A long, heated moment. "But I like your body even better."

I wonder if he's going to take us to dinner, or if he's going to take me right here, and if so, if I have the strength to resist him. Maybe I shouldn't even bother. Maybe I should just take the easy way out of this: give myself over to Charles. Forget whatever I thought I had with Malcolm. Live the life I was born for.

Instead, though, he drops my hand and starts driving us into town.

We listen to music on the way: a recording of Beethoven's piano suites that takes me back to the years I spent learning to play. My tutor had me listen to piano music while I did my homework for other subjects, while I was falling asleep and while I was getting dressed every morning. He wanted me to absorb the music, he said, to learn how the music *felt* as much as how it sounded. It's comforting to be reminded of those orderly days in this chaotic moment, and I'm slightly calmer by the time we reach the restaurant.

Charles picked a new place in the business district called Nina. It's Italian, and there's a bottle of one of my favorite champagnes waiting for us in a silver ice bucket at the table when we arrive.

"I called ahead," he says. "I hope you don't mind."

"Not at all."

He waves the maître d away and pushes my chair in himself, his fingers brushing against the tops of my shoulders so briefly I could swear it was an accident. It still makes the hair on the back of my neck rise and my pussy slick in my panties.

I've never been out to a dinner like this without my father before, and I feel thrillingly adult in my gown, with the most handsome man in the room paying all of his attention to me. This is the kind of place Daddy's business associates frequent, and I wonder how many men in here know him, or know me. How many of them will jerk off later tonight thinking about the way my tits look in this dress, or how I color up when Charles looks at me. Their dates are all looking at him, of course, and one way or the other I can feel most of the eyes in the room on me as I swallow my first glass of champagne in one generous mouthful.

There is no menu on the table, but that doesn't seem to be a problem, because everything's already ordered. The waiter brings us oysters and a salad that comes with a mound of caviar in the center, silky and glistening amid a bed of candied figs and tender, bitter arugula. I can't help humming around my first bite, closing my eyes in pure bliss. It's almost as if someone gave him an instruction manual for how to de-stress me on my worst days: first a glass of bubbly, and then a beautiful mound of exploding salty caviar.

"Isn't it gorgeous?" he says. "The first time I ate here, a colleague insisted. I was just back from Sicily, so I thought it would never measure up. How could it? But their chef was born there, and they import all of their ingredients. I think it's among the best restaurants in the city."

"Do you travel much?" I ask, taking a second bite, and then a third. It's second nature to make this kind of dinner-table small talk with someone, to feign interest in whatever man Daddy needs me to make nice with.

But it turns out I don't need to fake anything at all. "Quite regularly," Charles says. "My work demands it.

I've been almost everywhere, but I have to say, the Mediterranean coast has a special place in my heart. It has everything I love: good food and good open-ocean swimming. And then the rest of the country has all the art."

"I'll never forget the first time I saw a Titian in person," I admit. I've barely eaten today, and even a glass of champagne has loosened my tongue. "*La Bella,* in Palazzo Pitti. I was ten. I could have stayed and stared at it for hours. I'd seen reproductions, of course, but the real thing…it absolutely blew me away. I made Daddy change our plans so I could go to the Louvre after, and then to England, to see the collections there. The way he could paint skin and fabric…it's so sumptuous. There's absolutely nothing like it."

I blush harder, worried I've said too much, but Charles looks elated. "Titian is one of my favorites, too," he confesses. "That was the best part about working as a fine-art dealer—getting to spend time with so much beauty."

"A fine art dealer?"

"In my twenties," he says. "I wanted to be in acquisitions, but that wasn't to be. My talents took me into financing deals on the backend, so I ended up in banking like we all do." He speaks about his work dismissively, but I know that in order to be matched with me, he must be one of the wealthiest and most powerful men in the world—descended from a long line of them, in fact. I wonder how he got permission to spend those years on a personal project before he rejoined the family business. "But I still miss going to galleries every morning," Charles continues. "Hunting for something new."

"And do you still maintain a private collection?"

"Of course," he says.

From there, the conversation is easy, flowing between us as he orders an uni-topped pasta, a plate of grilled fish, and a spumoni that reminds me of why I ate spumoni every single day on that trip to Italy where I saw my first Titian. It's almost uncanny, how well Charles knows my favorite flavors: sea brine and grilled char and generous squeezes of citrus, followed by something light and sweet. By the time we're sipping tiny amber cups of amaro, I realize that I've hardly thought about Daddy, or Malcolm, or anything but Charles, in hours.

I'm light on my feet when we finally leave the restaurant, but the sight of his car reminds me that my home won't be mine tomorrow, and then I get heavy all over again. Charles must be able to see it, because he pauses in front of the car before circling around to the driver's seat. "What's wrong?" he asks.

I probably shouldn't tell him. But I'm tipsy and exhausted and softened by the hours we've just spent talking, so I confess. "Daddy heard I asked you for a break, and he thinks that means it's over between us," I say. "He's throwing me out."

"Do you need a place to stay?"

I hate asking anyone for help, but especially him—this gorgeous man who has offered me everything, only to have me tell him I need space and time to consider his offer. To consider him. "I do," I admit.

"My house has plenty of bedrooms," he says. "You'd be welcome to stay with me."

Relief washes over me like a waterfall, instant and wild. I don't have time to think through my response—I tug him over to my side of the car, which is sheltered by a parking lot wall, and drop to my knees in front of him.

With my hands on his hardening cock, I look up at him. When he nods slightly, I undo his belt and pants.

His cock is just as big as I expected, thick and hard in my mouth, and I relax my throat to let him all the way down. I look up at him as I suck him, and when he glances down and our eyes meet, I feel it deep in my core.

I apply everything I learned in training: deep suction mixed with the stroke of my tongue against his tender cockhead. My eyes widen as I strain to take as much of him as he needs. I know how to deepthroat as well as anyone in the world, and I demonstrate what his lessons taught me as best I can.

He only lets me do it for a few minutes, though, before he takes a gulp of air and pulls away, one hand cupping my jaw. I wonder if he's going to get me to my feet, fuck me right here, or maybe he wants to jerk himself off, come on my face and all over the dress he's been admiring all night.

Instead, his voice is deep and hollow when he asks, "Are you thinking about him?"

I'm glad I can't see my own face right now. "Who?" I respond, but my voice sounds too small.

He doesn't answer. He just puts his dick away.

Fuck, he *knows*?

"I'll take you home tonight to pack," Charles says, tucking himself back in. He sounds unruffled by the entire situation. "I'll pick you up in the morning. You only need your essentials. I'll give you anything else you're missing. And don't worry. I won't touch you. I'll wait for you to touch *me*."

With that, he turns and gets into the driver's seat.

I just stand there, frozen to the spot, feeling worse than ever. He knows about me—about Malcolm—how I feel and what I've done—and he's still taking me in, still caring for me. This man deserves more than me, and yet he seems to want me nonetheless. Do I even deserve him at this point? How could I have made such a terrible mess of everything?

Gage was right, I think, as Charles starts the car and steers us out of the lot. Everything with me is always far too complicated.

9

MALCOLM'S HOUSEKEEPER is the one to answer my knock, and I restrain myself from emitting a too-obvious sigh of relief. This will only work if I act like I was always supposed to be here.

"Hi," I say, trying to sound busy and bored. "I'm so sorry to bother you, but Malcolm sent me to grab something he needs for a client? I know where it is, I'll only be a few moments."

My carefully calculated affect must hit the right note, because she steps aside, saying, "I'm in the kitchen if you can't find it."

I wonder if she'll get in trouble when he finds out I've been here. Probably, I think, and honestly, maybe she should. Just because I'm wearing a Prada skirt suit I found at the back of my closet and speaking with authority, calling out her boss's name, doesn't mean I'm one of his employees. On the other hand, her credulousness got me exactly what I wanted, so I can't really complain.

I walk swiftly up the stairs, listening to the sound of my heels clicking against the dark wood as I ascend, and head confidently in the direction I hope will lead me to the master bedroom. I get lucky on my first try: it's not that hard, though, since it takes up most of the second story.

At first glance, it's exactly as I would have imagined it: an imposing four-poster bed sits atop a luxurious wool rug, and in the corner there's a gorgeous antique armoire with perfect teak grains around the curved edges. As in his kitchen, everything is organized, put away neatly in its place: his closet door closed and the top of his dresser gleaming under the recessed lighting overhead.

But then there are details I never would have thought to consider: the way that the desk is situated so that he can look out the window while he works, or the large bird feeder hanging from a nearby tree branch. There's a leatherbound copy of *Infinite Jest* on the nightstand, a bookmark reporting that he's a little over halfway through. Malcolm's house is a study in restraint and containment, so every visible personal detail feels like it speaks volumes, giving me dazzling but dangerous insight into who he is in his rare unguarded moments.

Starting soon, I won't have access to any of that anymore: not to his public façade or his private self. And whatever he thinks happened between us, I know one thing for certain: how I feel about it all. I'm ready to let him go, but not without a goodbye in my own words and on my own terms.

I find a piece of stationery on his desk, as well as a thick black Montblanc pen, which feels appropriately heavy in my hand. I let myself sit in his chair and watch a bird hover at the feeder—a jay, I think, quick and nervy, darting in to take a drink before it flutters away again—then I start to write.

Dear Malcolm,

Daddy kicked me out. I'm moving in with Charles. You were right. That's where I need to be. That's where I was trained to be. I know you were always looking out for me. So I'm going home to pack, and that's it. I just want to thank you for everything you've done for me, including and mostly not having feelings for me. You've both done right by me and fulfilled the contract you made with your client after all.

Juliette

I glance around the room one last time before I go, trying to savor the smallest things: the faint hint of a pattern on his navy quilt, picked out in equally navy thread; the rumple in his pillow where maybe last night he slept. The only other notable object in the room is a chessboard, displayed on a low table. The pieces are ivory, old, and beautiful, carefully carved but starting to show wear from thousands of hands pushing them across the board again and again and again.

The queen feels cool and solid and reassuring against my palm. I slip her into my pocket, one last souvenir, before I leave.

10

I WALK into my cottage with my mind on my packing. Charles said only the essentials, but it's not like I own a lot of basics—my whole wardrobe is special pieces, designer fantasies received right off the runway or else commissioned especially for me. I'm thinking I'll go for sentiment and comfort—my favorite PJs, maybe one of Daddy's old cashmere sweaters, and then of course my toiletries, many of which are products I've picked out specifically for myself over the years. I'm concentrating so hard on making a list that I nearly trip over Jane when I walk out the bathroom door.

I'm about to spill the story to her, starting with the sex with Malcolm in my bed and ending with my decision to stay with Charles, but she cuts me off before I can get two words out.

"I don't *care* about your latest drama, Juliette," she says. Her hair is pulled away from her face and her cheeks are flushed with anger. I've never heard her raise her voice to me before, and the sight of her fury makes me feel incredibly awful. How far have I gone if I've made Jane mad enough to yell at me? "You keep me in captivity endlessly while you flit around from expensive lesson to rich man and back again. You're not getting married. You're not moving out. You want to stay a child forever." She counts my sins on her fingers, and each one feels like a paper cut, flicking a tiny, discrete shiver of pain along my skin. "And I'm so tired," she continues. "All I want is my own life, but I'm chained to yours. Bruce is tired of waiting for me to wait for you and I can't blame him one little bit. Every day you hem or haw without a thought to how long I wait around to see if I'll be free before I can ask my boyfriend if he's free too. I'm almost always alone, but I'm never able to own my time."

"That's not—" I try to defend myself, but she won't even let me finish my sentence.

"Where's the lie?" Jane asks. "I don't get a thing—not even my time--until you're married, and my time is yours 24/7. So the longer you wait to commit, the longer I have to wait to do anything for myself."

I don't have a response, because she's right.

"It's going to be all right."

I'm about to explain that I'm moving in with Charles. I've cut Malcolm off with a note and she'll be free soon, but I'm interrupted by the sound of the doorbell.

I turn mechanically and open it. Only the shocks of the last 24 hours keep me from reacting. I'm drained, at this point, numb, and seeing Malcolm on my doorstep, perfectly buttoned-up and at his Masteriest, doesn't even surprise me. Of course this is what's happening now.

Jane stirs behind me. "I was just leaving," she says.

I can't let this conversation end this way, especially if I'm going to Charles's in just a few hours. "Jane," I say. "No. Malcolm. It's a bad time."

"No," Jane corrects. "It's a perfect time."

I stand between them, torn. Now that Malcolm is finally here, I want to throw myself on his mercy, beg him for another chance. Show him that I can be perfect for him. Show him that I can be everything he trained me to be. And anyway, he doesn't have to love me. He only has to keep me.

But if I do that, I won't be able to tell Jane that her life and her happiness matter to me. That she won't always be at my beck and call, dependent on his. But of course, that depends on disproving the first.

And there's no guarantee that will happen.

Malcolm speaks before I can decide what to say. "You have something of mine."

The chess piece. I was a fool to think I could keep a souvenir.

"You two deserve each other," Jane says, starting to leave.

Malcolm's eyes narrow. He seems surprised. I wasn't supposed to tell anyone about the fucking, not even Jane. But I did, and now he knows it.

It's not like it's the only way either one of us broke the rules.

"No." Malcolm's denial stops Jane in her tracks. "We don't deserve each other." He looks over her shoulder, to me. "I got your note. It was puerile and unconvincing. I saw you coming a mile away. But...I had an immediate reaction to what you wrote. I can't ignore it. It was..." He clears his throat. "There's an imbalance here, between us. There's always been and I've thought it scaled in one direction...but I've been looking at it in a mirror, Juliette. It's you—"

"Look," Jane interrupts with a break in her voice that hurts me, because it's my fault. "You don't need so many words to throw me under the bus, okay? I'm already flat on my back. Alone. Prospectless."

"There are no feelings between Malcolm and me." The words burst from my mouth. "None at all." I've heard him say variations on this sentiment ever since I met him, and more than ever since we started fucking, but coming from my own mouth, the words are scalding. If Jane's accusations were paper cuts, tiny, burning stings, this feels like I'm hollowing out my own guts—taking myself apart from the inside out.

He looks the way I feel. Scooped out. Broken. Shocked by what's coming out of my mouth.

What the hell did he want? Is this what it takes to get him to realize he has feelings?

All I had to do this whole time was tell him he meant nothing to save my friend some heartache? Chasing him was a mistake. I should have told him I didn't give a shit. Played the game. Led him around on a leash. That's the most helpful lesson he taught me, and I don't have to be schooled twice.

"It was just a fuck," I say, keeping my eyes on his. "Meaningless. He's a wonderful trainer, though, and I'd be happy to recommend him."

Jane surveys Malcolm with her brows in a knot, as if she can read the pain in his face as clearly as I can. Then she turns to me and I tear myself away from Malcolm to listen to her. "Are you sure?"

"Yes. He's nothing but a paid fuck. The best in town." I'm lying, but I'm also telling other truths. I never meant anything to Malcolm. I'm moving in with Charles, and her happiness is important to me.

"She's right," he says coldly. I glance up at him. The brokenness is gone. He is Master. "It was just fucking."

"Well," Jane says, crossing her arms over her chest. "I'm happy for you both. But *I* have feelings. And whatever you are or aren't feeling, you definitely did things. Bruce broke up with me. Everything is screwed and even if it wasn't, I've been living in the Newmont cocoon since I was a kid. I don't know how to even date. So, I'm never getting married thanks to this 'just fucking' thing that had nothing to do with me."

Malcolm seems to really see Jane for the first time in this conversation: I watch his gaze snap into focus as he truly becomes Master, a man who knows exactly how to train a woman, and who's worth his time and energy. She's no longer my paid companion, a guest star in our drama. He assesses her curves with professional acumen. Jane knows our world. She's alone. She's lovely and kind.

"Oh, Jane," he says. "Don't fret. I've got plenty of clients who'd be interested in a beauty like you."

Jane glances my way, and what else can I do? If she has a chance at the life I spent weeks throwing away, she should have it.

"Really?" she asks him.

"If you have the stomach for the lessons." He's looking at me, but he's so guarded and cold I don't know if he thinks I had the endurance for them or if I was a failure.

I hide my discomfort with a nod of support. I know Jane loves Bruce, but if she's already lost him, then Malcolm could set her up with a rich husband and it might solve things between us. We could even be friends again, but this time on the same footing, belonging to the same class. Maybe everything would be better, then.

"I do," she says. "Don't I, Juliette?"

"I think you do." I step out of the way. I will do my friend a good deed. Fix the mess I created before I go to Charles. "Malcolm, you should talk to her. Get started right away."

Malcolm comes in. I close the door behind him and go to the kitchen, thinking they'll have a nice interview while I pack for Charles. In the meantime, I'll think about all the times he said he didn't have feelings for me and I'll work on believing him.

We don't deserve each other.

He said it. He did not lie. I don't deserve a man I could choose.

I had an immediate reaction to what you wrote. I can't ignore it. It was...

It was what?

Juliette. It's you—

It's me...what?

"Get your clothes off," he says to Jane. "All of them. Let's take a look at you."

Wait.

I think it, but it won't come out because I'm stuck on questions I'm afraid to ask, because the answers can hurt Jane as much as they'll hurt me.

Jane hesitates, looking over at me.

"Do it if you want the lessons," I say. "It's okay. No feelings."

Jane doesn't hesitate. She unbuttons her silk blouse, sliding it down her shoulders before stepping out of her jeans. Her bra and underwear come off next, and then she's naked, her familiar body bare for Malcolm's assessing gaze. She's beautiful, the way she always is, her skin smooth and lovely against the flame of her hair.

I turn to Malcolm, and he's locked in on Jane, as if I'm not even in the room. He examines her with professional attention, taking in everything from the sheen of her hair to the tips of her toes. I hate watching him turn that spotlight intensity on someone else more than I ever could have guessed.

"You'll have to take some personality tests," he says. "Find out what you can offer a husband."

He runs the back of his hand over the peaked tips of her nipples, his mouth twitching with a smile when she blushes at his touch.

I cross my arms in front of my chest. It doesn't mean anything. This is his job.

"Generally," he continues, "we cater to a certain kind of client, with particular tastes. It's hard to know where you fit in without a lot of effort."

"I understand," Jane says. I wonder if she feels the way I do when he touches her—like his hands are the only thing in the world that matters. Like her skin is on fire. Like she might die of emptiness if he doesn't fuck her.

"Do you?" Malcolm asks, and pinches her nipple.

Jane groans, and then flicks her eyes over at me again, guilty.

I keep my face encouraging. She can do this. She should do this.

"I've heard about every one of her lessons," Jane says. "I know what this entails, and I'm ready to do whatever it takes."

"Well then. Put your hands behind your back and spread your legs."

She does it without question or protest. Her feet aren't quite eighteen inches, but she's not far off.

"Excellent," he says. "Now, let's see." He reaches a hand between her legs and strokes a finger along the seam of her pussy. Jane holds still, but she closes her eyes with evident pleasure.

"You're wet," he says. "That's good. How many men have fucked you?"

"Three," Jane says. Her voice is lower, now, husky with desire. I feel like I'm shrinking into the corner, merging with the wall, as I watch this scene play out. *This is the right thing,* I remind myself. *Malcolm needs girls, and Jane needs a way out of the life I've locked her into. Whatever happens with me and Malcolm, this is the right thing to do.*

Malcolm flicks her clit and says, "Good." He strips off his jacket, folding it neatly over the nearest chair. "Do you like getting fucked?" he asks her.

"Yes."

"I'll be the judge of that." He undoes his belt now, coiling it on top of the jacket. "Get on the table and lie down, face up."

He reacted to my puerile note in his heart. How? I want to know. I need to know. But Jane's hopping up onto the dining room table. I turn away. I can see her in the mirror, propping herself up on her elbows.

He said he had a mirror image of the power imbalance. He thought it was him calling the shots, but it was me.

Jane's legs are spread for my Master.

I sink down into one of the chairs in mute, stunned disbelief. He's going to fuck Jane the same way he fucked me the first time.

And I'm going to watch him do it.

I could say no. I could stop it because the mirror isn't reality and his heart—his reaction to living without me—is where I have power.

But that would steal a life from Jane and give it to a man who'll wake up in the morning and deny, deny, deny. I am so sick of his denials and his carelessness.

Malcolm pulls his cock out of his pants, and the first jolt of shock gives way to a searing sense of hurt. I've seen him fuck plenty of other women, but even the one in the skybox didn't get to me the way this is. I know it's for the greater good—my mind hasn't changed at all—but God, I feel like my heart is breaking.

"Wider," Malcolm says to Jane, indicating her pussy. "Use your hands. Offer it."

Jane lies all the way down on the table and reaches between her legs. "Like this?" she asks.

"The asshole, too."

"I've never done it there," she says, and for a second I wonder if this is how it ends: Jane refuses, and gets off the table. And then I don't have to watch Master fuck her with his perfect cock, and none of it is my fault.

Of course, that's not what happens.

Instead, Malcolm slaps her pussy and says, "Do what I tell you the first time."

That commanding tone goes right to my cunt. My body wants to respond; I want him to be using it with me. To be the only one he uses it for. I want to be the only whore who gets to have him like this.

But he'll never have just one, and even if he did, it

wouldn't be me. I know it. So at least I can let him help Jane.

From where I'm sitting, I can't see between her legs, but from the way her body shifts and Malcolm's clinically pleased look, I can tell she's done it.

I know that look. I thought that it was evidence of the undercurrent I felt between us. But apparently it's the look he gives every woman who spreads for him. It's part of his professional arsenal, not evidence of his personal desires.

"You have a pretty cunt, Jane," Malcolm says. He slaps it again, and this time, Jane groans. "I think I can work with it. What do you think?" He thumbs at her clit, gently, and then harder. "Do you want to learn how to be a perfect little slut?"

"Make me perfect, sir," she says, and I remember how he had to tell me say *sir*. To carefully, exactingly train me to do exactly what Jane's doing with instinctive ease.

He takes his cock and rubs it along her seam, gathering her wetness, teasing her with pressure. "I think you're really close already," he says, and whether or not he means it, I hear the unfinished corollary to that sentence: *as opposed to Juliette*. It took me weeks to get to where Jane is now. She's going to surpass me in no time. How long until he forgets me entirely?

"Please find me a client," Jane says. "I'll figure out how to pay you."

"Are you begging?" he asks.

"I am," she says. He's still rubbing himself against

her but not pressing in, and her breathing is getting ragged, her hips threatening to hitch themselves up just a little bit, to take what it is she wants. "Please teach me to be a fuck-doll. Make me a slave."

"I think we can break you in nicely." Malcolm looks at me in the mirror with an expression of provocation and a challenge as if to say *Stop me*. "Destroying what I fuck is job one."

Stop me before I destroy you.

But I can't. I won't. If I ask him to and he does stop, Jane loses. If he doesn't, it will be the final proof that he never cared about me, never felt anything more than simple lust when he looked at me. It will confirm, for once and for all, that nothing I could ever do—no amount of time or want or perfect behavior—would ever make me special to him.

"Do it then," I say, checking my nails to look bored. I know he's looking at me, waiting for me to stop it and declare my love. I can feel his expectations. "Get on with it. I have time-sensitive things to do."

I sit in my chair and glance at the mirror. Malcolm turns away from me and pushes his cock inside of Jane, fucking her with the same detached precision he used when he took my virginity. He looks like another man might while stepping onto a train, or signing a contract: interested but not invested. Half here and half somewhere else.

It still feels like every thrust is a dagger between my ribs.

It's even worse to see that Jane clearly loves the

feeling of his dick as much as I do; she's writhing and moaning on the table, completely unselfconscious as he buries himself in her, over and over again. I keep waiting for Malcolm to look at me again—give me something, anything—but his gaze is drifting somewhere on the wall in front of him. Even when he was fucking Trina in the ass at Gage's party, his eyes were locked on me the whole time. Now it's like I'm not even in the room. What he's doing isn't about proving a point to me; he's testing out Jane's pussy, giving her the fuck of her life, because it's his job.

This moment means nothing more to him than what it is.

And here I am, shattered by every stifled grunt.

Jane reaches for him, trying to pull him in closer, and he won't allow it; he captures her wrists neatly between his hands and pins them over her head. He keeps fucking her while he does it, metronome steady, and she sounds like she's on the brink of falling apart.

I glance up and something awful sears through my heart: I know that look on his face, too. I watched for it at the ballpark the other night. He's as close to coming as Jane is.

Jane goes first, thrashing and shuddering through her orgasm while Malcolm holds her wrists and fucks her through it. Her voice is rough with use when she cries out for him to give her more, keep fucking her harder, harder, *please*.

I can't watch anymore. I've felt exactly what Jane is feeling. I always knew he was capable of giving this kind of pleasure to other women—of course he was. He had to be. But to see Jane, who I love, who I've always loved, give him pleasure in return is too much. I don't want to know what he looks like when he's blissed out on the wetness of another woman's cunt. Especially my best and only friend's.

I get up quietly, trying not to distract either of them, and go to my room. But the table moves with every thrust, and I can hear them through the door, Malcolm ordering Jane to come again for him before he follows. He grunts his satisfaction, groaning his way through his orgasm, and I can't help making miserable comparisons. *Did he sound like that with me? The first time? The second? Was it better with Jane? Is he not even making the comparison because he barely remembers what happened between us?*

I'm curled up on my bed when I hear them separating, finally, the sounds of furniture being pushed back into place, the shushing on of their clothes. His footsteps sound on the floors, and then I hear him saying to Jane, "Meet me at my office at 9:13 a.m. tomorrow. Juliette has the address."

Of course he's going to make me give it to her. One last twist of the knife, a final bit of cruelty to make sure I'm completely and utterly wrecked. A reminder that my husband bought my place in his program, and I still failed out of it. Jane will get by on merit alone.

He promised me he'd never feel anything for me. How can I be so gutted by the fact that he kept that promise?

Jane knocks on my door, soft and hesitant.

"Come in," I call, so she does.

She's sheened with sweat, still, damp and radiant from her orgasms. Looking at her feels like looking directly into the sun. I keep my gaze focused on my comforter, with its sprigs of flowers set against a sky-blue background. It's based on a Gucci wallpaper I fell in love with in a Parisian townhouse a couple of years ago, and usually, it reminds me of how big and beautiful the world is. Today it just reminds me of things I used to hope for, and don't anymore.

"Can we talk?" Jane asks.

I force myself to look up. I will get this right, at least. "There's nothing to talk about," I tell her. "What I was going to say before was that I'm moving in with Charles. You could have gone back to Bruce if you wanted, but maybe this is better for you. Malcolm can…he can really change your life."

He certainly changed mine. In this moment, I'm still not sure whether for better or for worse.

Jane doesn't say anything, and I can't read the expression on her face. I can't help myself; I drop my gaze again.

So I only hear the sound of her footsteps as she turns and walks away from me.

11

Charles's house is beautiful. A romantic mansion on the coast with every classic touch paired with every modern convenience. The picture windows look down onto the crashing ocean, and wisteria winds around every doorframe, but you can set the temperature in the rooms with the touch of a button. The grounds are extensive, and I'll be able to play tennis in the mornings and then sit in the hot tub all afternoon. The foyer where he greets me is lush with roses in the peak of their bloom, and my future husband fills out his suit so perfectly it should be a crime.

But I see all of it through a veil of grief. I'm still shocked. Undone. Devastated.

I had been so certain—*so* certain—that I loved Malcolm, and that he felt something deep for me. But then he did the one thing that could prove he didn't, and never had. No man capable of love could have done what he did with a straight face. He even enjoyed himself. I saw the way he looked when he fucked Jane. It wasn't that different from how he looked when he fucked me.

This is why you're here, I remind myself. *Because Malcolm was a bad option. This is better. This is your future. And you will fall in love with Charles. You will.*

After we walk around the grounds together, Charles brings me into the kitchen, where a lavender buttercream cake is sitting on the counter, waiting to be sliced. It's my favorite, and I'm touched all over again by his thoughtfulness, his apparent ability to anticipate my every want.

It still tastes like sand in my mouth, though of course I don't tell him that. I try to seem excited and grateful. To be who I wish I was right now, instead of who I am, which is a shell of myself struggling to get through each moment.

"As long as you're here," Charles says when he's finished his own slice. "There will be some rules."

I nod. Of course. I'm glad, actually. I need some structure. Some routine. Something to cling to in order to get me through the next few days.

And also, as hurt and messed up as I am, I don't truly mind this gorgeous man telling me exactly what to do.

"You'll have my credit card," he says, sliding a black card across the counter to me. "No spending limit; buy whatever you want. But I will give you instructions about what sorts of outfits to purchase—shoes, lingerie, everything."

The card's plastic is comforting in my hand, a promise of a way to fill my hours. I wonder what he'll want me to wear. How he'll like me best.

My pulse picks up its rhythm.

"You may never close the door while showering or bathing," he continues. "You will accompany me to social events, and we may also host some here. When that happens, I expect you to be an immaculate hostess and a perfect date. Do you understand?"

"Yes."

"You'll watch porn with me when I ask you to," he says. "I know so much about your tastes—it's time you learned about mine. And we will be sharing a bed. But don't worry, Juliette. I won't touch you. Until you ask to be touched."

I want to think that will take a long time. He's moving so fast already… the guest room to the main room. I know I need a pause to nurse this broken heart. I wasn't lying to Charles about that before— I also know he is out of patience for me and mine. I don't want this to feel like just another lesson, or a rebound from my ill-advised feelings for Malcolm. But I also don't know how to change it.

I also know that the way he's set this up will lead to temptations I'm not prepared to resist, especially as upset and confused as I am. The idea of bathing in front of Charles—watching him watch me slippery and soaking wet—performing a perfect hostess role—and then climbing into bed with him to watch his favorite porn… There's no way I won't end up in his arms sooner rather than later.

I don't know how I feel about that. But this is my life now, so I try to greet it with a smile.

12

MASTER

BEHIND A LOCKED DOOR, a painting leans on the wall. I never hung it. That would have admitted too much. Even owning it is a mistake.

Until recently, I never made these kinds of mistakes.

The image on the canvas is indelible. The girl in the portrait is naked, marked with the slime of a man's cum. She is used, degraded. In training to be a faceless, worthless whore.

And yet, her blue eyes and heart-shaped face are defiant. She hasn't broken. She's impatient. Restless. Alive.

That day, I thought she'd never break. It started to scare me eventually: the silk-thread strength of her, the way that, even when she looked fragile, she could absorb so much without snapping. The fierce way she started to believe in the idea of us.

But nothing is invulnerable, and she did, finally, break.

I was the one who broke her. It's not the victory I thought it would be.

I've been trying to convince her to let me go for weeks, and at last, I've succeeded, but that's not what it feels like. Instead, the phrase that keeps occurring to me is: *I lost her*. Worse, I pushed her into another man's bed.

No.

I don't care about his bed. I don't care where he puts his cock. Wasn't I the one who taught her that fucking is just fucking? What bodies do doesn't necessarily mean anything.

Instead, it's her heart and her soul I'm thinking of. He owns those now, and that's what I cannot bear. All of that vivacity, that tensile strength, is his domain.

I don't make blunders. I don't miscalculate. Not with women.

Perfection is my goal, and I reach it, every time.

But if buying that painting was my first mistake, letting her go was an even bigger one.

Because even with the portrait locked in the closet, I can feel her watching me. Her gaze is penetrating, angry, skewering. It's a question that demands an answer. And it reminds me that however far I run, I'll never escape her, or the things she's made me feel.

Master Class continues with Lesson Nine: Master

I was hired to do a job.
There was nothing unusual about the client.
But there's never been a girl like *her*.
Juliette is pure innocence.
I want to claim every bit of it for my own, to dominate and control and own her.
Mastering my feelings is my job now.
Because if I give in, I will destroy us both.

Get Master

ALSO BY RAVEN JAYNE

MASTER CLASS

A collection of dirty, erotic novellas

Lesson One: Obey

Lesson Two: Tempt

Lesson Three: Take

Master Class: First Three Lessons

Lesson Four: Submit

Lesson Five: Offer

Lesson Six: Play

Master Class: Lessons Four, Five, Six

Lesson Seven: Trust

Lesson Eight: Break

Master Class: Lessons Seven and Eight

Lesson Nine: Master

Lesson Ten: Choose

PAIGE PRESS

Paige Press isn't just Laurelin Paige anymore...

Laurelin Paige has expanded her publishing company to bring readers even more hot romances.

Sign up for our newsletter to get the latest news about our releases and receive a free book from one of our amazing authors:

Laurelin Paige
Stella Gray
CD Reiss
Jenna Scott
Raven Jayne
JD Hawkins
Poppy Dunne
Lia Hunt
Sadie Black

ABOUT THE AUTHOR

Two NYT erotica authors got together and thought up a dirty little story. You're welcome.

Made in the USA
Columbia, SC
25 October 2024

45058581R00126